American Short Fiction

PUBLISHED IN COOPERATION WITH
THE TEXAS CENTER FOR WRITERS
Rolando Hinojosa Smith, Director,

AND WITH THE SOUND OF WRITING,
A SHORT STORY MAGAZINE OF THE AIR,
BROADCAST ON NATIONAL PUBLIC RADIO,
Caroline Marshall, Executive Producer

AMERICAN SHORT FICTION

Volume 1, Number 3, Fall 1991

LAURA FURMAN
Editor

BETSY HEBERT
SUSAN WILLIAMSON
Editorial Assistants

JOHN KINGS
Managing Editor

Editorial Advisory Board

ARTURO ARIAS   CYNTHIA MACDONALD
DAVID BRADLEY   JAMES MAGNUSON
ALAN CHEUSE   JAMES A. MICHENER
FRANK CONROY   ELENA PONIATOWSKA
ELIZABETH WARNOCK FERNEA   JUDITH ROSSNER
TONY HILLERMAN   LESLIE MARMON SILKO
FRANCES KIERNAN   TED SOLOTAROFF
JOSEPH E. KRUPPA   WILLIAM WEAVER
OWEN LASTER   WENDY WEIL

UNIVERSITY OF TEXAS PRESS

AMERICAN SHORT FICTION, established in 1991, is published four times a year by the University of Texas Press in cooperation with the Texas Center for Writers and "The Sound of Writing," a short story magazine of the air broadcast on National Public Radio. The editor invites submissions of fiction of all lengths from short shorts to novellas. All stories will be selected for publication based on their originality and craftsmanship.

STYLE   *The Chicago Manual of Style* is used in matters of form. Manuscripts must be double-spaced throughout.

MANUSCRIPTS AND EDITORIAL CORRESPONDENCE   Please send all submissions to: American Short Fiction, Parlin 14, Department of English, University of Texas at Austin, Austin, Texas 78712-1164. Manuscripts are accepted only from September 1 through May 31 of each academic year. Please accompany submissions with a stamped, self-addressed envelope.

SUBSCRIPTIONS (ISSN 1051-4813)   Individuals/$24.00; Institutions/$36.00. Foreign subscribers please add $5.50 to each subscription order. Single Copies: Individuals/$7.95; Institutions/$9.00. Send subscriptions to: American Short Fiction, Journals Division, University of Texas Press, Box 7819, Austin, Texas 78713.

"Le Traiteur" by Jude Roy and "What's New, Love?" by Wright Morris are published courtesy of "The Sound of Writing," a short story magazine of the air broadcast on National Public Radio.

Design and typography by George Lenox

Cover photograph by Carol Cohen

CONTENTS

THE EDITOR'S NOTES

To some readers the idea of fiction being edited or fact-checked may seem peculiar and wrong-headed, and even as futile as trying to rearrange acres of bluebonnets. But most published fiction has been edited, either lightly or heavily. The job of the fiction editor is to question what doesn't seem to work by itself or to fit with the whole, and to leave alone what does work, which can be a delicate intellectual juggling act, for in any good story the pieces work with one another or not at all.

The final arbiter, of course, of what is right and what isn't must be the writer. One of the pleasures I've had so far in editing the first three issues of *American Short Fiction* is watching a writer come up with an unexpected and completely logical adjustment to a sentence or a paragraph so that it no longer is a problem but takes its place in the story. Only the writer can come up with the right solution. Sometimes the best thing I can do as an editor is to recognize that what I thought should be changed or moved is just fine where and how it was originally.

Fact-checking fiction sounds like an oxymoronic process, and possibly nonsensical. Still it has its real uses and can strengthen a story as much as good editing can. The rule of stepping back and letting the writer decide applies equally to both processes.

The first time Rebecca Morris's character Anne Martin appeared in print was in *The New Yorker* in a story called "The Good Humor Man." During our last go-round of editorial questions and answers, Ms. Morris mentioned that the *New Yorker* fact-checker ate quite a few Good Humor bars, I suppose to verify the accuracy of the names and flavors of the ice cream bars in the story. For *American Short Fiction,* Rebecca Morris went out in twenty-degree weather to find suntan lotion to confirm that it did smell like coconut oil, not the vanilla she remembered.

As our readers might imagine, we have no fact-checking staff at *American Short Fiction.* But we do read our stories carefully; and the editorial staff, the copy editor, and the proofreaders work diligently to insure that if a place name is mentioned it is spelled correctly and is in the correct hemisphere. If an ice cream bar is said by a writer to have a certain crunch, we are willing to test that fictional proposition against the real thing.

This kind of mild fact-checking may seem to be an obvious task for any publication, along with setting a consistent style for punctuation, but a publication of fiction must bend with the wind of fiction. We do not publish journalistic or scholarly accounts in which the journal and the writer stake their credibility on verifiable facts. The important facts of fiction are subjective, emotional, and individual, and hard to verify except as a subjective, emotional reader. If a phrase or date—that is, language or fact—strikes us as possibly wrong, we check it as we can and always question the writer. Then it is up to the writer to make the final judgment call. Sometimes the writer may insist on an eccentric spelling or manner of punctuation, and this we also try to respect, within the very broad limits of the style we are establishing for *American Short Fiction.*

We work with the writer for consistency within the world and language of the writer's story. The fiction writer works in the no-man's land of imagination, where, paradoxically, it is essential to be accurate in language and fact about events that have never taken place. ⌘

SUSAN FROMBERG SCHAEFFER

CHICAGO AND THE CAT

ometime during the night, the huge wooden clockwork in back of the sky ticked, moved once, and now the weather changed. The heat was gone and the humidity with it. A crisp wind blew in the hopsacking curtains his girlfriend Marie had made for him. He refused to call her his *significant other.* The phrase was ludicrous, and he never knew how significant she was, or how other. In conversation she remained, therefore, his girlfriend, although the phrase seemed, among his friends, antique, as did his habit, in spite of his training, of attributing human purpose and intent to events in the mechanistic world. The world might well be a tapestry knotted together by intersecting forces and vectors, but when he was not in the laboratory, he preferred to see everything as if it were animate and full of purpose, so that each unpredictable thing might, at any moment, decide to alter its nature, and perhaps in so doing, change the significance of the entire design.

The wind blew the navy blue curtains into the room so that, for an instant, they floated up toward the ceiling like the last long, thready clouds of the night, and then dropped down, every thread in the fabric visible. There was a sharpness to the air that smelled like apples, and the

American Short Fiction, Volume 1, Number 3, Fall 1991
© *1991 Susan Fromberg Schaeffer*

wind rustled dryly in the oak leaves, a sound that reminded him of his mother's taffeta slip as she dressed for a wedding one night, in the winter, long ago, in New York. Summer was gone. Autumn had come for it, plunged its sharp teeth through its sluggish, long throat and carried it off. He looked with regret at Marie, who sat on the blue couch, pressed against the armrest, in the same position she'd been in for hours, weeping without sound, occasionally lifting her hand holding a handkerchief to her nose, then lowering her arm and letting it rest once more across her stomach. She was wearing jeans and a peach-colored brassiere, and over it she wore her white chenille bathrobe. He must have interrupted her, she must have been doing something, getting ready for something, when she asked him, "Do you still love me?" and he said, he said it immediately, because he had been asking himself the same question for months, for almost a year, "We never meant this to last forever." She put down her mascara and began weeping, put her bathrobe on over her jeans and brassiere, and sat down on the couch where she wept still.

He was curiously unmoved by the sight. He thought odd things. When she moves out, will she take the curtains? She was entitled to them. She had made them, but he loved them more than she did. He saw the morning light coming through the fabric's rough weave, and thought, Once we were like those threads, so close, and now we are not. Will she take Figaro, our small black-and-white cat? He had been her cat, but now the cat cared only for him. Figaro was nowhere to be seen, probably asleep on the dining room table in the back room. He had an image, so vivid as to be a hallucination, of two people, himself and Marie, coming into an empty laboratory. Each of them carried a white bakery box tied with string. The string had been made by twisting together red and white strands of thread. In each box was the love each one felt for the other. The love itself, its substance, was ensconced in the box, and rested on a white paper doily cut to look like lace; it resembled a cake. Its substance was crystalline and it was very clear, but it was sticky to the touch and somehow unformed. It reminded him of sap on the bark of a tree, sap that had not yet hardened. Except for a huge black table, the room was empty. At each end of the black table was a gold scale, and he knew immediately that they were to take their boxes and weigh them, thus settling once and for all the question of who loved whom more. Outside, the wind had picked up strength, and blew the curtains in and up once again. They rose suddenly, like a flock of startled pigeons. Perhaps if pigeons were deep blue, not battleship gray, people might love them more. He turned his attention to the gold scales. Each placed his box on the scale, and as Marie looked at her scale, and then her box, she began to weep. Did her box weigh more or less than she had hoped? It occurred to him that he was so tired he was dreaming with his eyes open. He waited for her to say, "You never loved me." Once she uttered those words, this scene would come to an end. She would stop weeping. Either they would begin to discuss what came next, or one of them would fall asleep, but in any case, Marie would move, get up, decide whether she wanted to be dressed for day or for night; they would not be frozen in their poses forever. Or, he thought, she might try to kill me. She was looking at him now out of narrowed eyes. The eyes of snakes, he thought, must look like that. "You never loved me," she said. In the laboratory, the bakery boxes turned into pigeons—or perhaps they were doves, they were so white—flew up from the scales and out of sight. The laboratory had no roof.

He smiled at Marie. He was always pleased when events confirmed his expectations. It was a satisfactory outcome, as when an experiment confirmed a hypothesis. Next she would say, "Why are you smiling?" and she was beginning to say something when the phone rang. "I'll get it," she said, jumping up to answer the telephone, as if to say, I'm still of some use here. Once I'm gone, you'll have to answer your own phone and make your own excuses. You better think twice. She always covered the phone with her hand and whispered the name of the caller so that, should he so desire, he could shake his head, and she would say that he had not yet come in, was asleep, would call back later, but now she stood still, her white robe over her jeans, the receiver of the telephone thrust out in front of her. She had become inanimate.

He took the receiver from her. His mother's voice came through the small holes. What was she saying? He felt Marie's hand on his arm. With her other hand, she was vigorously drying her eyes. "Dead?" he said aloud. "Dead?" His mother was saying disconnected words, *sudden, no pain, a blessing,* and then parts of sentences, "so sudden he didn't have time to ask for you," "tomorrow, someone will pick you up at the airport, just tell me what flight you're taking, he wants to be buried in Florida. That's where he lived," and he thought, Why not Chicago? It's colder in Chicago. He'll last longer. He said some things. They must have been satisfactory because his mother let him hang up. "I'll go with you to the funeral," Marie said.

"No," he said. "I'll go alone."

"Oh," she said. "You'll go alone." She knew his dread of death. She sat down on the couch. Not again, he thought. We're not starting that again. "So," she said, "if it's over, you'll want me to move out." She watched him. "I'll start packing," she said. When he nodded, she shook her head. "You bastard," she said, getting up and going into the bedroom, from which, in seconds, issued the sounds of drawers yanked open. He knew, without getting up, that the bed was now covered with her possessions. He lay down on the couch, on his back, looking at the cracks in the ceiling. "The trouble with you," his mother used to say, "is that you're too sensitive. You're too sensitive and too fussy. You have to compromise. You can't be such a perfectionist." He didn't know if he was sensitive or if he was a perfectionist, but in that instant, he knew there was something wrong with him, something missing.

"I'm sorry about your father," Marie said, standing over him.

"Mmmmm," he said. The higher the sun rose, the colder it became.

"Oh, well," Marie said.

———

"So that," he told his mother, "was the end of Marie." He thought his mother would do more than smile or nod; she had liked Marie, but Marie was not Jewish and was therefore unacceptable. He looked at his mother, disappointed, but then reminded himself that his father had just died and that his mother was now a widow. Who knew how widows reacted to anything? And this might not be the best time to tell his mother about Marie, not while they sat in the second seat of the black limousine driving to the cemetery. His mother's hot, dry hand rested on his wrist. She stared straight ahead. He looked out the window and thought how ugly it was here in Florida, flat and green and hot, the frying pan of the country, while in Chicago it was cold and at night frost nipped at the earth. If his father had to die, then he had died at a good time. The semester had not yet begun; there were no exams or papers. His father's death had rescued him from Marie. She could not very well ask him to stay with her and miss his father's funeral. Altogether, his father had picked a most convenient time to expire. He suspected his mother did not think so, but then she seemed calm. All her conversation had, so far, concerned finances, although she had said that she intended to stay in Florida because she had built a life here.

Built a life! What was she, a mason? But then his mother always tended to talk in cliches. *Don't throw out the dirty water until you have new.* Of course it was not right to be annoyed at his mother who was now a widow. When she stopped being a widow, then he could become annoyed at her. But did people ever stop being widows? It occurred to him he was not thinking properly.

The cemetery shocked him. Proper cemeteries had headstones that stood at right angles to the ground, mausoleums, statuary, winged angels carved from marble; they resembled little cities, had, from the highway, silhouettes of great cities. A cemetery seen from the highway defied your sense of scale, or at least disturbed it. This cemetery had stones set in the earth, a name and a date carved on each; flat, shiny gray stones he at first mistook for paving stones so that he tried to walk on them to avoid the muddy earth. It must have rained the night before. He hadn't noticed. His mother, who saw him stepping on the stones, jumping from one to another, said nothing, as if she saw nothing odd in his behavior. Perhaps she thought this was the way sons behaved whose fathers had just died.

The rabbi was saying something, but then rabbis always said something and in any event, he couldn't hear him. He felt the pressure and heat of his mother's hand on his arm, and he began to see a line of people coming in to a low gray granite cottage where a dead man was laid out on a large oval mahogany table. "Sorry for your trouble," said each visitor passing the widow and her daughters. "Sorry for your trouble," until it became a chant, and watching, he was outraged. "Sorry for your trouble," as if the visitors were commenting on a toothache rather than a death. When his mother tugged at his arm, he understood the funeral was over and that they were to return to the car, and as they walked, he wondered why he had just attended a funeral in Ireland, one that someone had described to him some months back, instead of his own father's funeral, at which he had been, as anyone who could read minds would know at once, absent.

His mother was regarding him, smiling sadly. "It hasn't hit you yet," she said.

"It hasn't?"

"It hasn't hit me either."

"I think it's hit you," he said.

He didn't like the way she looked at him now. "If it doesn't hit you, you'll be sorry," she said. Wasn't that wrong? Wasn't she supposed to say, "If it hits you, you'll be sorry?" The heat had unhinged him, the heat and these stepping stones. His mother would be all right. She was one tough cookie.

———

Marie had gone. There was no trace of her. It was as if she had viciously scoured herself from the apartment. She had, however, left the curtains, and Figaro was asleep in the middle of the bed waiting for him. The neighbor had fed him in his absence. He sat down on the bed and contemplated Figaro.

He had never had a pet before Figaro. His mother, who often boasted that her kitchen floor was so clean that a brain surgeon could operate upon it, and whose tragedy, in his opinion, was that no such surgeon had ever come to her door saying he had an emergency and needed a sterile kitchen floor, had feared dust, germs, animal hair, the sharp claws of animals shredding the beautiful tapestry fabric of her chairs. He had once brought home a parrot, and for the few weeks it lasted in the house, he had sat next to its cage, trying to teach it to say, "Hello, Daddy," so that, when his father came home from work, the parrot could greet him. He knew his father well enough to understand that a bird with a kind word for him at the end of the day would have a permanent place beneath their roof.

However, the bird did not learn quickly, and after several weeks, his mother read an article about a recent outburst of parrot fever in Jamaica, and the bird was returned to the store.

Figaro had arrived with Marie, the Mother Teresa of cats. She found him when she took her cat into the veterinarian's to be put to sleep. "This is a wonderful kitten," the vet said, bringing out a black kitten he held by the neck. The cat hissed and spit and struggled while Marie inspected him. He had an asymmetrical streak of white fur that bisected his face and cut across his nose. He looked, as everyone noted, demented. Marie picked up the cat and he walked across her arm, used his nose as a wedge to lift her coat, and went to sleep above her breast just beneath her shoulder. She had decided to take the cat when the vet reminded the receptionist that the woman who had brought in the kitten and who had paid its bills had asked to approve the person who would adopt it. The woman was duly called and within fifteen minutes came in, brushing snow from the collar and chest of her coat.

"Where *is* the cat?" she asked.

Marie opened her coat. Only the cat's rear end and tail were visible. At the sound of the woman's voice, the cat turned, peered out from the depths of Marie's coat, and then retreated.

"Oh, well, he loves you already," the woman said.

"I love cats," said Marie.

"Her cat just died," said the receptionist. "Of diabetes."

"Diabetes?" the woman said. "I didn't know cats got diabetes."

"They do," said Marie. The kitten was absentmindedly chewing on one of her fingers.

"You know why he's here?" the woman said. "There's this gray cat who leaves her kittens in our boiler room. We found him down there. He was sneezing, his eyes were gummy, he was a mess, so we started feeding him. We wanted to bring him in here but he wouldn't let us near him. So we waited until his eyes stuck together and we dropped a carton on him. We got him here just in time."

"Just in time," said the receptionist. "He had pneumonia."

"So he's not such a friendly cat," the woman said. "I mean, first it was a boiler room, and boxes dropped on him, and then it was a cage and things stuck in his rear end and needles through his skin. You know."

"A survivor, that cat," said the receptionist. "If you see what I mean."

Marie took the cat home. For the first week, it hid beneath her legal bookcase, coming out to eat when she left the room. Then it began to lie down on the living room rug, as far from her as possible. She always spoke to the cat, said hello when she came in, told the cat she would be back soon when she left. Occasionally, she read aloud to the cat. One morning when she awakened, she was surprised to find the cat wedged into her side, asleep on its back. When she tried to scratch its stomach, the cat attacked her wrist and she walked around with Mercurochrome stains and Band-Aids for a week. She named the cat Figaro.

He met Marie when the cat had begun to sit, cautiously and suspiciously, on the couch with her. Its fur was now so shiny the light reflected from it and the fleas that had bitten Marie so hungrily were gone. It was no longer a kitten, but neither was it a cat. It was thin and long and leggy and its only interest, as he saw it, was in food. When they fed the cat, it would eat until the plate was clean and then cry for more. They fed the cat incessantly and ignored its cries only when the cat's stomach bulged ominously. At such times, the cat looked as if it had swallowed a shoe box.

"*Can* cats explode?" he asked Marie.

"Don't give it any more," she said.

Marie usually fed the cat, although he often stood over

Figaro and watched him eat. Still, he was the one the cat followed, the one onto whose lap the cat jumped, the one of whom Figaro was jealous. If he read a book, he had to hold it high in the air so that the cat could not lie down on it, and when he held it up, tiring his arms, the cat would stand up on his hind legs and pull the book down with his front paw. When he went to bed, the cat came with him. When it was cold, the cat tunneled under the covers and slept on his ankle. If he went into the bathroom, the cat scratched at the door until he let him in.

"Why me?" he asked.

"It's love," Marie said.

"I don't love him," he said.

"But you will," she said.

He looked at Figaro, lying on the bed. He had come to adore the cat. The cat seemed to him, in its calm surveillance of all that occurred, almost omniscient. Its green glass eyes, so clear and transparent, were like pools of the purest water, so deep that, when he looked into them, he thought he could almost see into the brain that perceived the world. When he spoke to the cat, he believed there was nothing the cat could not understand. When he gave the cat commands, it obeyed them. If he told the cat to flip over on its back, the cat did, waving its paws in the air, waiting for its stomach to be scratched. If he held his hand over the cat's head and said, "Stand up," the cat stood up and held onto his fingers. He explained his experiments to the cat and the cat understood them. He knew the cat was a pure soul. He knew beyond a shadow of a doubt that the cat loved him. Once Marie had pretended to hit him with a newspaper and the cat had jumped on her leg and begun to rake at her skin with its back claws.

As he stroked the cat, it seemed to him that the cat did not look well. He tried to remember: Was it feed a fever, starve a cold? Starve a fever, feed a cold? Until the cat seemed healthier, he would not feed it. Figaro stretched, yawned, and as if approving of his decision, climbed onto his lap. He lay back on the bed and the cat crept onto his stomach, rising and falling as he breathed.

When he came home from the lab the next day, the cat seemed better but more nervous. Figaro flew around the room. The cat crept into the paper bag he put down on the floor and sprang out waving his front paws. Figaro would crouch down in the middle of the rug and then run madly around the room, his wide, round eyes on him. He thought, He is more playful because he feels better. He considered feeding the cat, but decided that, to be on the safe side, he would wait until morning.

In the morning, Figaro once again seemed unwell. He decided that his lab assistants had the experiment he was running well under control. He would stay home with the cat. As the days went by, he read book after book. For the first few days, the cat protested, as was his habit, either lying on the book or standing up to drag it down, but eventually, the cat grew resigned and lay across his legs without disturbing him. By the end of the week, he had to carry the cat over to his dish of water, and as Figaro drank, he would look up at him from the floor, reproach in his eyes. His lab assistant called and said things were going well. He decided to remain at home with the cat until he was better.

"You have your whole life ahead of you," said his mother. "I have nothing. All I have left of him are his golf clubs. You could call more often. I'm always here."

"What's the weather like?" he asked his mother.

"What's the weather like?" his mother asked, her voice rising to a shriek. "This is Florida! What should the weather be like? It's hot! It's always hot!"

"No hurricanes?" he asked.

His mother hung up. He stared at the receiver in disbelief. He was making conversation. She always liked to talk about the weather. Why did she only have his father's golf clubs? What had she done with his clothes? If she'd given away his clothes, why didn't she give away his golf clubs and make a clean sweep of it? But then she was a widow. He didn't understand widows.

"I'm not a widow!" his mother shouted at him when he next called her. "I'm still your mother!"

"You're a widow and you're my mother," he said. Widows, apparently, were irrational. His mother hung up. Perhaps widows did that—lost their tempers, hung up on their sons.

Figaro, meanwhile, absorbed all his attention. The cat was listless. His ribs showed through his fur. When he pulled back the cat's lower lip, his gums looked pale. When he went into the kitchen or to the bathroom, the cat sighed and got down from the couch, following him, but when he first landed on the floor, his legs seemed to wobble beneath him. Lately, he seemed to stagger as he walked. He took to picking up the cat and carrying him wherever he went. When he lay on the bed, the cat sucked at his fingers or licked his skin. Occasionally, the cat, as if apologizing for his weakened state, reached out to pat his arm.

"Why can't you come down for Christmas?" his mother demanded. "All the other children are coming down for Christmas. It's not as if these are normal circumstances!" His mother, he believed, kept actuarial tables of the number of visits children made to their parents in Florida. He said something to that effect and the line went dead. When she ceased being a widow, he thought, she would cease hanging up.

When it became apparent to him that the cat was going to die, he spent every moment with the cat. He no longer read or watched television. He watched the cat. He wanted to observe the exact instant when it ceased to breathe. He wanted to know when the cat went from being something living and warm to something dead and cold. He began drinking cup after cup of coffee in order to stay awake. The cat now slept most of the time. When it awakened, it would look around, turning its head from side to side, but not lifting it, to see where he was. Then the cat would stretch out its small hot paw and rest its paw on his arm. He stroked the cat rhythmically and incessantly, and softly, because the cat's ribs now showed so prominently through its fur. He imagined the full weight of his hand on the cat would be painful and so, when he touched the cat, he did so lightly and carefully.

The doorbell rang one day and when he opened the door he saw Marie standing on the landing. She waited, expecting him to invite her in, and he thought, Figaro was her cat, too; I should let her see the cat, but then he thought, The cat is so weak the excitement would kill him immediately. He muttered something about having someone in the apartment, but if she'd wait a minute everyone would be decent. Marie flushed and said she had better be leaving. He went back in to the cat. Figaro had managed to pick up his head and was staring fixedly at the door as if he were hoping for rescue, but of course he had been too weak to go to the door. Figaro had no choice. That was what it meant to be dying, he thought. The dying had few choices and then they grew weaker and had no choices. They wanted to live and they struggled to live but they could not choose to live. "She's gone," he told the cat, and the cat lowered his head and lay still. He was still breathing. He lay down next to the cat and fell asleep. When he awakened, the cat was still breathing.

As it happened, he was awake when the cat ceased to breathe. He pressed his ear to the cat's chest and could not hear his heartbeat. He saw that the eyes of the cat no longer focused. Still, the cat moved, odd, convulsive movements.

Wake up, he told the cat. Get up. I'll give you something to eat. But the cat did not wake up and he understood the cat had died. As he stroked the cat's stiffening body, he began to cry, and he sat on the edge of the bed through the night, stroking the cat and weeping. In the morning, he put Figaro in a carton and took him to the lab where he would be cremated.

When he went home, he called his mother and said perhaps he might come to Florida for Christmas after all. He asked his mother whether or not she still had his father's golf clubs, and if so, could he use them. As he talked to her, his eyes wandered to the almost-full carton of cat food next to the refrigerator. How long had it been since he'd fed the cat? Almost two weeks. It was astonishing to him that an animal could go that long without food.

"So," said his mother, "it's finally hit you."

"What's hit me?" he asked.

"Look, I don't want to talk," his mother said. But she did not hang up.

———

He thought of this now because he was staying for the weekend with friends in Maine. They had a huge field-stone house and when he had driven up to it, his two children fighting in the back seat, his wife still reading the directions scribbled on the back of an envelope, a black cat had been sitting on the front step. A lightning-like stripe zig-zagged from its nose to its chin and when he saw the cat he felt a surge of joy that rose like a warm tide from his stomach and flooded his chest. He helped the children unload their suitcases and he carried in the golf clubs in their old red leather golf bag—the leather had cracked and had the texture of old, weatherbeaten skin—and then went back for the boxes of cake his wife had baked, but his attention was fastened to the cat. As soon as everyone was inside, he announced that he had a headache and asked if anyone would mind if he went up to bed. No one minded. The children were running down the road to the ocean and his wife was running after them. The cat was standing in front of him, and he swooped down upon the cat and carried it with him to the bedroom his hostess had pointed out. He took the cat inside and closed the door. He put the cat down on the braided rug and lay down. He pulled the brass bed's feather comforter over him. Milky white light poured in through the curtainless window. He lay on his back, his hands folded beneath his head. Eventually the cat jumped up on the bed and lay down on his chest, staring into his eyes, just as he had known it would.

"It's you," he said to the cat. "You're back."

The cat purred and flexed his claws. "My mother died," he told the cat. "Not long ago, but long enough." The cat crept forward until his cold nose touched his own. He began to stroke the cat, and as he did, he began to weep. "I'm sorry," he told the cat. "You're not angry?" The cat reached out, touched his cheek, and flexed his claws. He tapped the cat's paw gently and the cat, purring louder, retracted his claws. "She's been dead eight weeks," he said, and the sound of the cat's purr, ever louder, made him sob, so loudly he had to turn on his side and bury his face in the pillow. It seemed to him that the least thing made him cry, and he remembered his mother saying, not long before her death, that when he was younger he never cried and she had worried what would become of him. She was old; she spoke in non sequiturs. *You look like your father,* she said. The cat, as if he were walking on a rolling log, managed to stay on, settling on his hip. He thought, as he wept, that from a sufficient distance he might look like a grave covered in snow, and the cat the carving on top of the stone. It is because of Figaro that I have anything, he thought, poor Figaro, who starved to death, and as he thought that, he felt sleep settling on him, erasing him, and he understood the fog wanting to erase him, as he understood how the houses, the lawns, and the sea would feel when the fog gathered its strength, thickened, and erased them all.   ❧

SUSAN FROMBERG SCHAEFFER was born and resides in Brooklyn and teaches at Brooklyn College. Ms. Schaeffer is the author of numerous novels and collections of poetry and short stories. Her most recent novel is *Buffalo Afternoon*.

LE TRAITEUR

My father was a *traiteur,* a healer, and the believers trusted him and came to him whenever they were sick.

Mr. Theophilus Jogneaux was a believer. When he visited our house with his son, I sat at the kitchen table eating cookies and milk. My father asked them in and poured Mr. Theo a cup of coffee. The boy stood next to his father and eyed my cookies with large dark eyes. I offered him one, but Mr. Theo shook his head when the boy looked up at him. My father waited until Mr. Theo was seated at the table and had sipped his coffee before asking him what was wrong with his son.

"My boy got a nasty sore throat, Monsieur Leclerc. You think you could treat him?" Mr. Theo spoke Cajun, in a slow nasal drawl. His voice was soft and respectful.

My father asked Mr. Theo's son to come closer. The boy did as he was told and stood with arms at his side, his body rigid and straight. My father had gentle hands. He ran them along the boy's throat and neck, poking gently here and there. Whenever he hit a sore spot, the boy flinched. But he did not make a sound.

"Get my lantern," my father told me, and I ran and grabbed the lantern hanging next to the front door. I lit it

American Short Fiction, Volume 1, Number 3, Fall 1991

and handed it to him. He adjusted it and told the boy to open his mouth. Again the boy did as he was told and quietly allowed my father to shine the light in his face. I could see the lantern light reflected from the boy's dark eyes. They were wide and fearful.

"Get me a spoon, son," he told me, and I brought him one from the kitchen drawer. He used it as a tongue depressor. He said nothing. After a few moments of staring into the boy's mouth, he pulled back and traced a cross over the boy's lips with his thumb and forefinger.

Like magic the fear disappeared from the boy's eyes.

"Stand right where you are, son. Don't move," my father said, and he walked into the bedroom. I watched from the kitchen table. He cut a section of string about a foot long. He tied thirteen knots in the string and said a silent prayer over each knot. His lips moved, but no sound came through them. The prayers were secret.

I checked to see if Mr. Theo and his son watched, too, but Mr. Theo gazed into his coffee cup and the boy looked up at the ceiling.

My father returned.

"Son," he said to the boy. "This string has the power to heal your sore throat. I believe that with all my might. But it won't work unless you believe it, too." My father let a few moments of silence pass. "Do you?" The boy said, "Yessir," and my father tied the string around his neck. He opened the boy's mouth and blew three times into it and traced another cross over the lips when he was done.

"You have to keep that string around your neck until it comes off by itself. If you do that, then you'll never have a sore throat again." After another cup of coffee, Mr. Theo and his son left.

My father never charged for his services.

"That's a fact," he said when I asked him about it. "A *traiteur* don't have the right to charge."

"Why not?" I asked. Something in the way the boy looked at my father made me curious.

"It's an old, old tradition passed on to me by Jacob Patout while he was on his deathbed. Someday, before I die, I'll pass it on to you. It's an honor to be chosen, son. It's got little to do with me or you, though. It's in His hands. And theirs, those that come to be healed. You have to be a believer to be healed. And a believer's not scared what'll happen. He knows in his heart. It's in his eyes. The eyes will always tell you."

It was Mr. Theo who drove my father to the charity hospital in New Orleans when he passed out at the cotton gin. The doctors told him he had cancer and it was too late for him to expect miracles. They didn't exactly say that, but he saw it in their eyes. He told me so when he came back. There was one chance, he said, and that was to visit Mr. Elcid Thibodeaux, a broom maker and healer who lived five miles away in the woods off the Issacton Road.

We had made the trip many times before. My father liked to hunt squirrel in the woods behind Mr. Elcid's shack. But this time it took longer than usual. He had to stop and rest often. He did not talk much, and when he did his words came out in gasps as if he were struggling to talk and breathe at the same time.

Mr. Elcid sat in his rocker on his front porch whittling on an oak sapling, a handle for one of his brooms, when we walked up his dirt lane. Several finished brooms stood together leaning against one corner of the porch next to a few old cypress boards. Job, Mr. Elcid's Catahoula hound, barked and growled when he saw us, but stopped when Mr. Elcid slammed his foot on the porch. He put his knife and the sapling aside and stood up slowly. He squinted at my father.

"Seth Leclerc, you old dog, you. Haven't seen you since squirrel season two years ago. What brings you to my front porch?" My father shook hands with him and sat next to the steps. He struggled to breathe and his face looked haggard and drawn.

"Give me a chance to catch my breath, Cid."

Mr. Elcid nodded and sat back down in his rocker. It was impossible to tell how old Mr. Elcid was. He had gray hair the color of moss and a sharp little chin that jutted out from his toothless mouth. Two milky brown eyes, almost the same color as Job's, watched my father from behind the mass of wrinkles that was his face. He turned them on me and I saw the worry in them.

"How you doing, boy? How's school?" he asked after a while.

"Fine, Mr. Elcid. I start the seventh grade next month."

"The seventh grade, eh? Boy, aren't you the smart one. You going to be a doctor or something?"

"Nosir," I answered. Job rubbed against my leg and I bent over and petted him. Mr. Elcid turned his eyes on my father again.

"Ready to talk yet, Seth?" My father took a deep breath and looked up at Mr. Elcid with his pale blue eyes. They were moist and troubled.

"I'm afraid I come on some business, Cid," he said.

"What business can you have with me? You need a broom?" Mr. Elcid grinned, exposing his gums. My father did not grin back.

"No, Cid. I need you to treat me."

Mr. Elcid lowered his eyes and let them travel up the length of my father's body, stopping at his eyes.

"Well, you sure don't look too well. What's the matter with you?" He sat up in his rocker.

"The doctors in New Orleans tell me I got cancer. I don't know too much about it, but they tell me it eats up your insides until there's nothing left. They said I had a chance, but they didn't believe none of that. They said one thing, but their eyes said that I was as good as dead."

Mr. Elcid stood.

"Stand up there in front of me, Seth. Let me have a look at you."

My father stood. He was almost a full head taller than Mr. Elcid. Mr. Elcid ran his hands over my father's chest. He looked into his eyes. He sat and waited until my father was seated before speaking.

"It pains me to say it, Seth. Me and you go back a ways. But there's nothing I can do for you."

I looked at my father. I saw the fear in his eyes. He looked down at his feet. When he spoke, his voice was soft, almost a whisper, almost pleading.

"I was kind of hoping, Cid. Kind of hoping." I reached out and touched his pants leg. He never noticed.

"Seth, things change. People know more now-a-days. Them *docteurs* from New Orleans, they know about this cancer. They got pills and medicine and Lord knows what-not to fight it. You know what I mean?"

"I know," my father whispered. "But none of that stuff is going to work. They so much as told me."

"Me and you, what we got, Seth?"

"Faith."

Mr. Elcid said nothing. He picked up his knife and sapling and began whittling again. My father stared off into the dark woods. He picked nervously at a splinter in the porch. Job scratched at a flea.

"Seth," Mr. Elcid said after a long silence. "A few prayers and a string aren't going to work on this."

"It was never them that worked anyway, Cid."

Mr. Elcid stood up and walked to the edge of the porch.

"How can I treat something I don't understand, Seth?" He looked up into the sky. His pointy chin bobbed up and down as he spoke. "My papa taught me how to make brooms. 'People'll always need brooms,' he told me. He was wrong. People use vacuum cleaners now and all kinds of things I haven't got no idea about. Oh, a few old-timers still come by to buy one of my brooms, but that's mostly because they want to chat with me." Mr. Elcid turned his eyes on my father. They were shiny and moist. "Seth, me and you, the things we do and believe, people don't need them anymore. The vacuum cleaners do a better job. And if they can't do the job, then my old brooms sure won't. *Tu comprends*, Seth? You understand what I'm saying?"

"*Je comprends*, Cid."

"We're like old Job, Seth." At the mention of his name, Job stood, stretched, and slowly made his way to Mr. Elcid's side. "I trained him to hunt wild boar but there aren't none left around these parts." He ran a hand along the dog's back. "Soon there won't be no Catahoulas, not Job's kind, leastwise. What'll people want with a dog bred to hunt wild boar when there aren't none left?" Job walked over to my father, who scratched behind the dog's ear. Job curled up next to him. "Do you understand what I'm saying, Seth? *Tu comprends?*"

"*Je comprends*, Cid." My father looked at the dog for a long time in the silence that followed as if he were trying to decide something.

Mr. Elcid did something very strange. He cried. No sound came out, just tears, two of them that slowly trickled down from each eye and disappeared in the furrows of his face. My father stood and placed a hand on Mr. Elcid's shoulder.

"*Je comprends*, Cid," he said softly.

"I got the power to heal, Seth. But how can I heal something I don't understand. Something like this cancer—something that eats up your insides. How can I fight that, Seth? How?"

"*Je comprends*, Cid."

Mr. Elcid raised his hand to the sky, palm upward, and brought it down and laid it gently on my father. He took his thumb and forefinger and traced a cross over his chest that ran from his forehead to his belt buckle and from the left shoulder to the right shoulder. Then he disappeared into his shack and returned with a string, which he tied around my father's neck. There were seven knots in the string.

"It's all I can do, Seth."

My father caught my hand in his. "It's time to go, son." His eyes were shiny and moist, but there was no fear in them anymore.

"Yessir," I said. "Are you going to die, Daddy?"

"Not really, son." He squeezed my hand.

I looked back once. Mr. Elcid snatched a cypress board from against the wall and laid it across his lap. Job curled up at his feet.

My father died in his sleep a few weeks later, Mr. Elcid's string still tied around his neck. He never did make me a *traiteur.* I never asked. I saw the pain in his eyes and never asked.

The funeral was a small one. A few people followed the hearse to the cemetery outside the town. I looked around for Mr. Elcid at the burial, but I didn't see him. At the head of my father's grave, though, stood a cross made of cypress. And inscribed on it:

SETH LECLERC

1909–1961

LE TRAITEUR QUI VIVE TOUJOURS

Mr. Theo and his son were at the burial, too. They stood outside the small circle of mourners. As we were leaving, they walked up to the gravesite. I stopped and watched as Mr. Theo removed his hat. His son stood next to him, head bowed. Mr. Theo said something and the boy looked up. I noticed the string, still tied around his

neck. I tried to see his eyes but he never faced me. I wondered what was in them as he gazed at my father's coffin.

Someone tugged on my arm and I left. I never did see
the boy's eyes but I imagined they mirrored my own—
shiny, moist, and filled with sadness because we were
believers. ✺

JUDE ROY's short stories have appeared in *The Southern Review, The Best
of Lafayette, The Southwestern Review,* and on "The Sound of Writing"
on National Public Radio. He has a master's degree in English from the
University of Southwestern Louisiana in Lafayette and a master of fine
arts (fiction) from George Mason University in Fairfax, Virginia. He
teaches at Clemson University.

REBECCA MORRIS

WAPAKONETA

When the Baltimore & Ohio stopped in Wapakoneta, Anne Martin was the only passenger to get off. The train pulled away, diminishing rapidly down the weed-fringed track, leaving her stunned and blinking in the July sun. She stood alone on the gravel siding. The backs of her knees still smarted from the hot plush seat and her suitcase lay slanted on its side where the conductor had dropped it down to her. They don't waste much time over Wapakoneta, she thought.

The noon sun beat straight down; the sky was blue and cloudless. Anne reached for her dark glasses, balanced above her forehead, and slid them forward onto her nose; the brown-glass tinted waves of heat and dust were still rising from the deserted track. Hitching her suitcase, she walked down the gravel siding toward the station house, crossing a patch of burnt grass. The door of the waiting room stood open, but the ticket window was shuttered and there was no station master in sight. Beyond the station, the ground sloped away to a sparsely graveled parking area and the back entrances of one- and two-story buildings. Anne started down the grade, dragging her suitcase through the weeds and Queen Anne's lace. Three cars were parked at angles, their metal hoods baking in the sun.

American Short Fiction, Volume 1, Number 3, Fall 1991
© 1991 Rebecca Morris

She passed them, feeling gravel sift under her sandals. Running along the buildings was a dirt alleyway banked by high grass and parked delivery trucks. Further on, the river curved and she could see the gray metal trapezoid of the bridge rising above the trees.

There's the Auglaize River, she thought, at least I know where I am, I'll end up at the bridge. She walked down the alley looking at the rear entrances of stores, trying to remember the town as she'd last seen it: Woolworth's, Penney's, Western Auto. . . . She'd spent her childhood summers here. Milk cans glaring in the sun were stacked shoulder-high against the back wall of the dairy and a sour, cheesy smell wafted through the screen door. We used to come here to get ice cream, she remembered, resting her suitcase in the dust, watching the flies buzz around the screen. I could go in and telephone but I'm almost home now. Once I get to the bridge, it's only a few blocks.

She had told the aunts not to meet her. Fredonia still worked as a secretary in the local machine-tool factory, although they must have known she was three years past retirement age; she had worked there since she was twenty. And Alma Rose, who had retired and might have met her, was recovering from a cataract operation. Neither aunt had ever married and they still lived in the house where they had been born. "I've sublet my New York apartment for two months," she told them when she called from Akron the evening before, "and I need a quiet place to stay for a while and finish some work."

Over the phone she heard Fredonia saying to Alma in the background, "It's Emma Anne in Akron." Then loudly, "Emma Anne, how's your mom and dad up there? We haven't had a letter for a month." Her father was the aunts' younger brother. "This certainly is a surprise for us, Emma Anne. Rose and I were just playing Scrabble and I said, I wonder who could be calling us at this hour." It had been nine-thirty.

"Look, Aunt Doe," Anne had said, "I won't be any trouble. All I want is a place to rest and work on my thesis. I could set a card table up in the front parlor and not bother anybody. There isn't room for me at home, not since they moved to the apartment. Anyhow, I thought it might be nice to be in a house again."

Anne lifted her suitcase, scattering pebbles, and continued past the dairy toward the river. At the end of the street was the haberdashery that her grandfather once held a half interest in. He had died long before she was born, but the store was still called Reade & Foltz when she was a child. Somewhere there was a photograph of her grandfather and Mr. Foltz behind the counter. Had her grandfather had a mustache? I've got to get Alma to show me the albums, she decided. I'm coming home. It's been a long time.

She was approaching the river now and could see the yellow water of the Auglaize moving slowly past its flowering bank. Insects buzzed under the hot weeds at the water's edge and the fume of the river lifted suddenly in a sluggish wave, hitting her nostrils like a slap. Anne stopped, resting her suitcase in the weeds. The rich spoiled smell of the river rose on the sun all around her. Further along the bank, tall trees cast shadows on the water. The last time she had seen that river, she'd been a child, hair flying as she dashed through the high slicing weeds, an angry tomboy pursued by her own fear of growing up. She had been eleven that summer. The summer she fell out of the pear tree. I'm old enough to have a child of my own, she thought, looking at the water. I wonder why it's so yellow? It was always such a yellow river.

————

When she turned up Elm Street, the house was on the corner, white and square, looking no different. Anne carried her suitcase over the lawn and up the back porch steps. There were five doors into the house, but everyone always entered through the kitchen. Anne peered through the screen door: "Aunt Alma?" She opened the door, feeling the screen sag, and let it bang loudly behind her. Anne stood in the kitchen looking about; the wooden cabinets had been painted white but the lead-topped sink still stood beside the stove. The kitchen smelled faintly of flour as it always had. Anne crossed to the cabinet and pulled out the slanting wooden flour bin. The flour was still kept there, but now it lay sealed in a commercial package. She remembered her grandmother standing in front of the stove, framed in light from the window, reaching over to pick out a handful of flour for gravy. She let the bin rock back into place, hesitating to open the other drawers. As children her cousins and she had always gone straight to the string drawer on their arrival to see if their "treasure" was intact. There should have been a biscuit tin with metal jackstones—forty-two of them, she remembered—a tin kazoo, and her grandfather's silver badge from the Wapakoneta Volunteer Fire Department.

Dear God, she thought, I haven't seen any of them for years. They were always there. I don't want to know. The door to the pantry was standing open and she crossed to it.

Inside the pantry the trapdoor was pulled up, leaving a gaping square through the floor. Alma must have gone down to the cellar. Anne approached the opening cautiously and looked down. The trapdoor had always been dangerous. Her grandmother had forgotten it was open and stepped over the edge when she was eighty-seven and still doing the cooking. She had lain at the bottom with a broken hip for two hours until the aunts had come home from work, and although she died at ninety-two, she had never been quite as active again. They'll probably both go like that, Anne worried, looking down. "Alma, Aunt Alma?"

Along three walls of the pantry were shelves stacked

with tins and preserves, quart mason jars with homemade pickles and short, wax-topped glasses of apple jelly. Anne stared at a blue sugar canister with a dented lid. *That's older than I am.* It had always been filled with homemade cookies, thin ones with floury edges cut out of dough with an upturned water glass. She reached out to open the tin.

"Emma Anne," her aunt's face appeared, a white circle in the dark below. "Why, I didn't hear anyone come in." The face grew in circumference beneath Anne's feet as Alma progressed up the steep stairs. Light glinted off the thick rimless glasses Alma had always worn. Her aunt's body heaved upward step by step through the floor, reaching Anne's knees.

"Hello, Aunt Alma," Anne said, prying the tin open. It was full of Oreos.

St. Theresa: The Little Flower, Men of Maryknoll, Damian the Leper, The Keys of the Kingdom, Our Lady of Fatima. . . . Anne was looking through the glass door of the sitting room bookcase after supper. She remembered them all; she had read each one several times as a child. Fredonia was outside hanging dishtowels on the line, having carefully spilled dishwater over the peonies to discourage ants. Alma moved about setting up the card table for fan-tan.

"Aunt Alma," Anne said turning, "have you kept up the scrapbooks?"

Her aunt set the cigar box of pennies that they used for poker chips on the table and began counting them into piles. She looked up through her heavy lenses. "Well, I've saved everything, but I haven't pasted any of it for years. I meant to do it when I retired, but my eyes aren't what they used to be." She sighed.

"Can I take a look tonight?" Anne asked, turning the key in the glass bookcase door.

"What in heaven's name can you want in that bookcase, Emma?"

"Oh," Anne turned the key back. "Nothing, I guess. Just habit. We used to open everything, didn't we? Do you remember the time Mary Lou and I locked Evaleen in the little attic under the eaves?" Anne laughed. "Remember when Doe caught us prying the lid off the cistern?"

"Little Evaleen," Alma said. "You and Mary Lou were so mean to that poor child."

"She was a tattletale," Anne said firmly, "and a drag. Those Shirley Temple curls."

"You were both jealous."

"Weren't we, though? Everyone made such a fuss over Ev because she was the youngest. I had pigtails and Mary Lou looked like a blimp. We would have cut those curls off, but Lou was always afraid of Aunt Bridget. Little Evaleen," Anne mused. "You know we tried to set her on fire once."

"Emma Anne!"

"Well, we didn't *succeed*." Anne sat at the card table. "I really liked Ev the last time I saw her—at Lou's wedding. Anyway, Lou turned out to be the family beauty. Ev's hair went straight later. Have you seen them lately?"

"I remember whenever you and Mary Lou wanted anything you used to make Little Evaleen do the asking."

"She had her uses," Anne smiled.

Alma continued. "Mary Lou and Jack were down over Easter with Mark, Patty, and Little Mike. Mary Lou's expecting again in November."

"Has she got three now?" Anne asked. "We never had much in common after we stopped coming here in the summer. I haven't seen them since I moved to New York."

"You ought to live at home with your mother and dad," Alma said. "They worry about you. Doe and I were so happy to hear that you finally decided to come home."

"Only for the summer," Anne interrupted quickly. "I just got tired of the crowds, and I haven't been to Akron since they sold the house."

"Five years," her aunt said putting her lips together. "I think it's a disgrace, Emma, the way you choose to live all alone so far from your family."

"Aunt Alma," Anne protested. "They have their own lives. I'm grown up. Anyway there isn't room for me now. Alma, I've lived in New York for the last five years. Ohio isn't my home anymore."

"Your home is where your family is. . . . "

Fredonia appeared in the doorway. "What's this Emma Anne is saying?" She came in slowly, carrying three saucers of ice cream with chocolate sauce, and set them on the card table. "I thought we might like to have a 'dope' before we get started."

Anne smiled at the familiar Wapakoneta term. "I'm not sure I remember how to play." She spooned into the melting ice cream, watching chocolate syrup fill the indentation. The aunts' spoons clicked in their saucers.

The clock above the bookcase ticked through the pause.

Anne looked up uncomfortably. "The house does seem quiet, though. There were always so many of us those summers. I've never been to Wapak when Grandma Reade wasn't here."

"She had a very happy death," Doe said, "and the last sacraments only two days before the end. The six o'clock mass tomorrow is our mass—a memorial mass for Mom—although we generally do go to the seven. We get a ride home with the Farrs."

Anne had not come home for her grandmother's funeral. She had told her parents that she couldn't come; that her presence at the graveside would do her grandmother no good anyway. She hated family burials, which inevitably ended in a great spread of food laid on for the out-of-town mourners. The truth was, she supposed, that she'd been afraid. She might have had to explain her life. Someone might have asked her where James was. She should have gone though, simply to spare her parents embarrassment. Anne hadn't been to church for five years. The aunts went to daily mass—as did her parents, and as she had all through her childhood. Anne looked up, realizing that Alma was talking.

" . . . remarkable the way she kept all her faculties right up to the very end. Mom always said she intended to die at home; and she breathed her last right upstairs in her own bed." Alma fanned herself with a folded newspaper from the chair. "That last week, when the doctor said she might go any day, Doe and I took turns staying home from work to look after her. But Mom waited and died on the Saturday—so we were both with her to the last. And don't you know, at the very end, I swear she looked straight up, past us, as if she were seeing something there that we couldn't see. . . . "

Doe broke in quickly, "They say that at the hour of death, if you die in a state of grace, God lets you see your guardian angel."

Anne looked at her aunts, who were both fanning themselves in the silent room, and felt suddenly very hot and defeated. "Yes," she nodded. "Yes, I've heard that you can."

———

Anne carried the scrapbook into her grandmother's bedroom and dropped it in the middle of the bed. The upstairs was hot and the air hung in layers with a dry, brown-wood smell from the eaves. Both screened windows were open but no air stirred. She switched off the hanging light bulb and dragged the bedside table lamp closer. On the wall opposite, a picture of the Sacred Heart looked down from a wide black frame. One of its hands pointed accusingly to the thorn-wreathed heart flaming out of its breast; the other was raised in benediction over her head. As a child she'd been terrified of that picture. Now she turned to meet its baleful stare and raised her hand, returning the blessing, then she looked about. Her grandmother's bed had a high headboard flush with the ceiling and there was a marble-topped washstand lined with framed snapshots of grandchildren. In front of these lay a hairbrush and her grandmother's black rosary, neatly coiled.

Anne crawled up onto the big bed, feeling the mattress sag, and opened the bulging scrapbook. Alma's scrapbook was a family history—one her aunt had begun thirty years ago—of family papers, photographs, and snapshots, embellished with captions in colored type Alma had cut from magazines. It was nearly five inches thick now and loose papers trailed from its pages. As children, Anne and her cousins had begged to look through it. She opened to the middle where her generation began to see if anything new had been added and smiled at the familiar baby photos. Above hers Alma had pasted a blue butterfly and the words OUR EMMA ANNE. Mary Lou had gotten a frame of gold stars. She turned the pages looking at snapshots: Lou staring out of her baby carriage. Anne in a Dutch bob pedaling a tricycle. Ev's birth. The three of them one summer, lined on the porch steps, squinting into the sun. Anne tried to remember a smaller size of her own flesh. How had it felt? But the years had passed forever, stopped briefly by the chance of someone taking a snapshot.

Ev in her first communion veil, programs from Lou's piano recitals, Anne a frowning Campfire Girl. Lou growing slim. Ev beginning to look nervous. "HIGH SCHOOL GRADUATION." Her scholarship announcement and Lou's engagement photo. A single picture postcard of her college, then five pages: WEDDING BELLS, OUR MARY LOU AND JACK. Formal bridal photos, pressed white roses, snapshots—all the relatives eating cake. Anne turned the page: a new series of baby pictures begins, Lou's three. She hesitated; the next few pages should be for her children. "Nonsense," she told herself, and flipped past Lou's most recent child. Her own wedding stared back at her. James looking terribly young in his dark suit. Anne wearing her favorite green linen dress, holding an elaborate bouquet her mother had ordered despite Anne's objections. Like the record of *Lohengrin* her mother had put on the phonograph when they returned to the house. Small snapshots, all taken by her father. She and James were in graduate school and determined to spend little time or money on ceremony. The two of them grinned out of the snapshot, laughing at the fancy bouquet. "You fools," she told the photograph. Anne and James drinking scotch in the living room with Father O'Connell. They had finally married at St. Francis to please her parents, but in the rectory. Anne and James in raincoats, setting off to drive back to New York, mugging at the camera through the rain, water dripping off their hair. Anne waving—you could see her wedding ring. They hadn't ever told anyone it came from Woolworth's. That had been their joke; the very same ring that they'd used during the school year to check into hotels. The only real bit of sentiment in the whole ceremony.

"Nice try," she said grimly and let the scrapbook fall closed. The hot air hung heavy in the room; the bed creaked and sagged. Anne set the scrapbook on a nearby chair and switched off the light. From the window she could see the still, black leaves of the trees. There were fireflies in the garden below.

———

It was dark when they set off for mass. The sun had begun rising, drying the damp pavement as they walked. Crossing Wapakoneta Bridge, Anne watched the sun move down the surface of the water, yellowing the silt that flowed slowly above the deeper green. Bank grass, bowed with dew, leaned darkened points into the water. All around her, she could feel heat rising to dry the day. The sun's early burning rays slanted a long way toward them from the horizon. Standing on the bridge, Alma took out a handkerchief and wiped her brow, predicting that the day "looked like another scorcher."

———

St. Joseph's Church was dark except for the sanctuary lamp and some flickering votive candles banked before the side altar. Four nuns from the parochial school knelt in the front pew; as the bell tinkled to announce the mass, they rose in consecutive rustles and an old priest emerged from the sacristy. He was wearing black vestments and carried a veiled chalice. Anne stood with her aunts, reaching up to straighten the hat Fredonia had lent her. She'd tried to leave the house without one, but they'd stopped her on the porch, insisting she wear a hat, and pinned one of Doe's on her head, securing it with a long hatpin. The hat was straw, nest-shaped with velvet leaves and wisps of veiling. The hatpin pulled Anne's hair whenever she bowed her head, so she held her chin well up, knowing she looked comic with her long hair, cotton skirt, and sandals.

Incense from past masses floated in the hot recesses of the vaulted ceiling. Anne's nostrils pricked to the heavy liturgical smell. She knelt, watching the priest before the lighted altar, remembering early morning masses at the small convent boarding school she'd attended, mostly masses offered for the dead—dead the students did not know. At six A.M. in the candlelit school chapel they sang the Dies Irae on empty stomachs. Little girls in white chapel veils, watching clouds of incense rise in a yellow haze. "Dies irae, Dies illa, Solvet saeclum in favilla. . . ."

She had seen angels in that incense. Very often someone fainted.

———

They met the Farrs after mass in the church parking lot. Anne didn't know them, but on the walk to church her aunts had talked enthusiastically about the Farrs and their twenty-two-year-old daughter, Helen. They went to mass daily and always gave the aunts a ride home. Helen Farr was joining the novitiate of the Sisters of Mercy in September. All last year she had taught second grade at St. Joseph's school because there was a shortage of nuns. Alma had gone on much too pointedly about Helen Farr for Anne to bear. Helen had graduated from a Catholic college.

"I've never heard of Mercycrest," Anne said flatly. "Is it accredited?"

The Farrs were waiting by their new Buick. Anne bent down into the back seat with her aunts, removing the hat and hatpin. Her scalp felt hot and scratched. Helen Farr was sitting in front between her parents. Helen had short brown hair, freckled skin, and wore a shirt dress. I may be three years older than she is, Anne thought, but I look younger. She smiled at Helen Farr.

Mrs. Farr turned and addressed Anne. "It's so nice to finally meet you, Emma Anne, dear. Your aunts have told us so much about you. You're a teacher, aren't you?"

"No," she said, "I'm finishing a graduate degree at Columbia, in English literature. This summer I'm revising my thesis to submit in the fall."

Mrs. Farr looked confused. "Well, anyway," she went on, "your nice aunts here have told us so much about you and your clever professor husband."

Anne looked up sharply and caught sight of Doe's face and Alma looking worried. Oh, my God, she thought, they haven't told anyone I'm divorced. I've been divorced for two years and they can't admit it. The shame is too great.

"James is in New York," she said quickly. "He had to teach a summer school course—one of the men in the department got sick—so I came by myself." She looked around. Everyone seemed to accept that.

———

After breakfast, Anne carried the portable typewriter out onto the front porch and set it on the card table. The porch stretched in shadow across the house and around one side. Honeysuckle and thick-leaved vines twined over the railing to the roof. It was already too hot. Anne sat on the slatted porch swing and kicked off her sandals. The chains creaked slowly. She lifted her heavy hair to cool her neck. The metal thermometer by the door read ninety-two degrees. Through the screened window she could see Alma bent over the ironing board, alternately ironing and fanning herself, and she remembered her grandmother doing the same thing. "Aunt Alma," Anne called, "is that swimming pool by the playground—the one we always went to—still open?"

By lunchtime the temperature had risen to ninety-four. Alma carried a plate of egg salad sandwiches and a pitcher of lemonade out onto the porch where Doe, who had walked home on her lunch hour, sat on the swing in her stocking feet, fanning. Her white perforated health shoes lay airing below as she swayed. Anne sat barefoot on the porch steps, leaning against a post. She bit into a limp sandwich, spilling egg salad onto her bare knees, and jiggled ice cubes in her lemonade.

"They say at work that the heat's going to last all week," Doe announced. "It's been bad for the fair this year—people don't want to walk around in all this heat looking at animals. You can imagine the smell."

"Is the county fair on now?" Anne looked up. "We

ought to go some night. Remember the summer you took Lou, Ev, and me?" Anne laughed. "The time the Ferris wheel got stuck with Alma and me on top, and they couldn't start it up again."

"You rocked that seat deliberately, Emma Anne," Alma said. "Trying to scare me out of my wits. You always took such risks. Why, we must have stopped up there twenty minutes."

"It was lovely," Anne said. "We could see for miles, the whole fairgrounds. I couldn't have been more than nine. It was my first Ferris wheel." She smiled into her lemonade. "Real Americana. Later Ev's loose tooth came out in the saltwater taffy and she bled so much you took us all home."

"I don't remember that," Doe said.

"My memory is awfully good lately," Anne admitted. She sucked a wet lemon slice. "I'm beginning to feel about twelve years old again. I suppose that's because nothing has changed here." She drained the last lemonade from the glass. "I think I may just go swimming this afternoon. It's too hot to type."

———

She walked Doe back to work as far as the bridge, carrying her bathing suit in a rolled towel, then followed the river bank as it wound toward the municipal park and swimming pool. Only a few children were in the playground, swinging in the fierce sunlight. Anne crossed the worn grass, feeling patches of dirt loosen under her bare soles. Waves of heat glared off the metal sliding boards; they looked as if they would blister you at a touch. Beyond a row of swings, the ground sloped upward and Anne could hear the noise of the swimming pool before she saw it. Shouts and splashing; water sounds growing louder. The noon sun burned the edges of her dark glasses. The air smelled of chlorine and hot dogs. Anne pushed the sunglasses higher on the bridge of her sweating nose and started up the prickly grass.

The swimming pool, enclosed by wire playground fencing, was jammed. Children raced between the spread bodies sunning on the deck and flung themselves into the water. Spray arched through the air. As Anne drew level she could see the blue rectangle of water splashing with swimmers—pale at the shallow end shading to deep aqua under the diving boards. Red and white floats, strung beadlike across the moving surface, marked the drop-off. At the deep end children lined up, dripping, behind the diving boards. Along the cement deck groups of teenage girls sprawled on towels, talking and combing their wet hair. Oil glistened on their bare limbs.

As Anne watched, a boy sprang the high board, rising in burning outline against the sky before he jackknifed and cut the water in a bright explosion of drops. With shouts, small boys hurled themselves from both low boards. Water flashed up on either side. She shifted her towel, perspiring, and hurried along the fence to the bathhouse.

———

Anne stood waiting in the sun beneath the high board. The tanned legs of a diver were disappearing up the ladder. In a few seconds he would be above and gone. Anne gripped the tubing rungs and started up. Overhead the board dipped and vibrated. As his body cut the water, she saw his feet overthrow: too much arch. Clutching the guard rail, Anne pulled herself atop the platform and held tightly. She had always been a little afraid up here. The board was covered in rough cocoa matting and stretched over the water; below, the pool was bright aqua. Children raced and shouted on the deck. The sky overhead was drifting with clouds. Beyond the pool fence she could see swings in the playground and the baseball diamond. Distant fields stretched away to farmland, roads curved through summer weeds toward town. Through the familiar landscape, taking its time, the slow yellow water of the Auglaize River flowed as if it had all summer to reach Lake Erie.

Anne straightened, sucking in her stomach, and carefully paced to a few feet from the end. The sun was hot on her shoulders. I'm going to burn, she thought. The board dipped as her weight crossed the fulcrum. She flexed and began her approach. One, two—on the third step she hurdled, landing to force the plank down. The board dipped and recoiled, throwing her upward into the air. Rising, she saw the clouds move. Anne brought her arms together—the water was rushing toward her eyes.

Down, down through the cold green layers of water, she swam, silent and alone. Far above, sun filtered through the soundless water. She turned deep beneath the surface, arms moving in pale sweeps, and stroked quickly upward following her own air bubbles. Her face broke the sealed surface into the noise and splashing.

Anne shook the wet hair from her eyes and swam a fast crawl to warm up, dodging children, exhaling a cold wake of bubbles that pricked along her arms like ginger ale. Still moving, she swiveled onto her back to rest. The sun was beginning to slant west, marking afternoon.

Anne gave the pool a professional glance; she had spent her college summers lifeguarding at a pool in Akron. There were three guards on duty here. A boy and girl perched on guard chairs while another boy roved the deck, blowing his whistle at small boys who played water tag. The swimmers were mostly kids.

Anne floated, looking up at the sky, remembering Ohio summers full of long days. The sun shone in her face and chlorine stung familiarly in her nostrils. For four summers, she had sat high above the swimmers, water splashing below her tanned legs—watching the afternoon sun cross the Ohio sky and make a sundial of her high, narrow chair. She'd pulled out hundreds of children, but there had never been a drowning or a serious accident. I wouldn't like the responsibility now, she thought. Anyway she was out of practice.

Anne sculled, bringing her legs together on the surface. They looked pale against the sun-glazed water. She had learned synchronized swimming in college and swum in the annual water ballet. She tried several ballet legs, one after the other, each toe pointed toward the sky. Not bad. Anne sculled both knees toward her chest, and tried lifting both legs at once. She immediately sank. Coughing, she emerged; she hadn't expected that. She wished she had a noseclip to keep the water out. Determined, Anne shook the wet hair from her eyes and tried a few somersaults, then a kip, extending both legs—toes pointed—as high as she could, before heading toward the bottom. Carried by the momentum of her thrust, Anne plunged straight down through the water. As she descended she saw a child's face, not far away, watching. She plunged deeper and saw another child swimming toward her. Dark braids floated upward as the child came nearer. Anne bubbled and waved. The tinted pool bottom was close now. Anne dropped her legs and, flexing, pushed hard, straight up to the surface. Nearby, the two children emerged. They were both about eleven years old.

"That was . . . cool . . . ," the child with the braids gasped, treading water, bobbing up and down with the effort. The second child kicked closer, arms moving in short, splashy strokes. "What was that . . . will you do it again?" Her hair was cut short with dripping bangs and she was freckled. A nose clip dangled from a peach rubber band around her neck. The questions came in spurts between breaths: "Can't you show us . . . ?"

Anne motioned them to follow and swam to the side of the pool. Their names were Ginny and Judy, and they came swimming every day.

By five-thirty, the sun's rays stretched along the horizon, casting golden streaks on the water. Anne lay flat on the pool edge, arms and chest extended over the water, holding Ginny's feet as the child tried to arch backward in the water. Anne had somehow acquired two other pupils. They all splashed like a row of frantic seals, while she held their feet.

"If you bend your knees," she warned them, "it's going to look funny."

Judy's noseclip was passed from one child to another. Anne hoped none of them had anything contagious. They looked healthy. She also suspected that some of them should be going home to supper.

Judy climbed onto the deck and sat beside her, panting. "Will you be here tomorrow?" she asked. "Hey." She leaped up, spraying water onto Anne's back. "Ellen."

One of the lifeguards was approaching. She was very young, with cropped curly hair and a deep tan. The sweet, coconut smell of suntan lotion filled the air.

"Hi," the girl said standing over Anne. "Do you go to college?" Her whistle swung from her hand on a red-and-white lanyard, the kind children braided in camp.

In the water, Ginny gave a desperate sweep with both arms and succeeded in arching under without bending her knees. Anne gave a downward shove on Ginny's ankles to help, then let go. She stood up, rubbing her beveled knees. "Not really," she said. "I've been out of college for years. I'm grown up."

The guard stared at her.

"It's hard to tell when you're wet," Anne said. "And I am in graduate school." Behind them, she heard Ginny scrambling out of the pool.

"Oh." The girl twisted her lanyard around one finger. "I thought you might be—because you do synchronized. I'm going to Ohio State this fall. They have a synchronized program there."

"Her name's Anne, Ellen." Judy came between them. "And she comes from New York City."

"New York," the girl looked at Anne respectfully. "I didn't think you were from Wapakoneta."

Anne put her hands up to shield her eyes from the sun. "I'm visiting my aunts . . . Reade on Elm Street. I used to spend my summers here when I was small . . . years ago."

"I'm Ellen Foley," the girl said. "You're very good."

"Not anymore." Anne shook her head. "I'm out of practice." She picked up her towel from the wet deck and wrung it out. Water splashed on the cement.

"We have a swimming group." Ellen let the whistle unwind from her fingers. "In the morning before the pool opens. Bob's sister coaches us. She went to Ohio U.—they have synchronized—but she doesn't know any of the stunts."

"Who's Bob?" Anne asked, draping the wet towel across her sunburned shoulders.

Ellen and Anne began walking toward the bathhouse. Judy and Ginny followed, Judy hopping on one foot to jiggle water out of her ear.

"Judy, you're getting me wet." Ellen gave Anne a look. "*Kids,*" she said. Anne guessed she must be all of eighteen.

"Bob Fuller is the pool manager," she explained. "You probably saw him. He guards sometimes, but mostly he's in the first-aid room, that's the pool office. Bob's at Ohio State now. We date."

Two boys passed them, eating hot dogs. A strong smell of mustard lingered in the air.

"Are you going to be in Wapakoneta long?" Ellen asked.

"A while," Anne said. "I'm trying to type my thesis, but the weather's gotten too hot."

They walked along the deck, trying to place their bare feet on wet patches.

"You could probably teach us a lot," Ellen said. "Sue is

coaching the kids to help Bob. He has to put on a water show. We're supposed to have a public demonstration at the end of every summer for the Park Department. You'd like Sue—she's been to New York. She teaches in the junior high school. Sue's taking the show because Bob can't get anyone else. She has little kids at home."

They'd come to the bathhouse; Anne could hear the showers running inside.

Ellen paused, and looked at Anne hopefully. "Would you like to come tomorrow morning and watch?" she asked. "I could introduce you to Sue."

"Please," Judy danced from behind, circling on the hot cement. "Say yes, Anne. You can use my noseclip."

After supper, Anne cleared the table, finishing the remains of the meat loaf in the kitchen, dipping bits of it in catsup with her fingers. She had made lots of meat loaf for James in New York; it was cheap and certain. He called Ohio the Great Midwestern Meat Loaf Belt. Anne smiled, capping the catsup bottle, and piled up the stripped corn cobs. There had been fresh corn on the cob for supper and sliced tomatoes still warm from the afternoon sun. Alma was putting on the kettle to scald the plates. Anne pulled a stiff dish towel off the rack behind the sink. Through the back screen door she could see the sun slanting behind the pear trees. The pears were green and hard looking. It was absolutely still. Anne began drying a water glass.

Doe took a clean towel from the drawer. "You look as if you got some sun today, Emma. You can't be too careful. They say the sun can give you cancer."

"It will tan by tomorrow," Anne said. "By the way, one of the pool guards asked me to stop by tomorrow morning. They need help with their water show. The kids are putting one on in a few weeks and they want me to direct the synchronized swimming. Water ballet," she explained to the aunts. "I think I may just go see what they're doing—if it's this hot again tomorrow."

Alma looked at her.

"One of the guards said she knew you from St. Joseph's," Anne added. "Ellen Foley? The pool manager was young; his name is Bob Fuller."

"Your dad went to school with the Foley boys," Alma said. "Fuller?" She turned to Doe. "Aren't they the ones who used to have the other dry goods store? I don't think they're Catholic," she told Anne.

"Well, I think I will go tomorrow," Anne said. "If only for the practice. I haven't done any serious swimming for years, but it doesn't seem that long." She looked out the screen door. The sun had set and the pear tree flamed.

Doe crossed to the cupboard. "Do you see James up at Columbia?"

"Yes," Anne said. "I see him. He's married again—you knew that, didn't you? He's been married for two years. I don't know her."

"You were married in the church," Alma said. "What God has joined together. . . ."

"James wasn't Catholic. Look, Aunt Alma, the divorce was his idea. I didn't want it. He left me for someone else. For God's sake, Alma, he's been married for two years now and I don't *even know* her."

"You're still married in the eyes of the church," Doe said gently. "We know how you must feel. I'm surprised that you stay at that school."

"I started a degree at Columbia," Anne said. "I can't transfer now. Anyway I don't want to. Columbia's a huge place, Doe. There are more students going to Columbia than there are people in Wapakoneta."

"That may be, but I don't see that all your education has made you happy." Alma poured kettle water across the dishes. Steam rose from the scalded plates. "Mary Lou never went to college and she seems very happy."

Anne picked up a plate, feeling the hot china burn through the dish towel. "Lou was always happy. When she was little she called all her dolls Patty—so what does she call her firstborn. . . ."

"Patty is a good saint's name," Doe said.

"You didn't even play with dolls," Alma reminded Anne. "You were always running wild or reading."

"What you mean is that I haven't any children."

Alma looked up. "I didn't say that." She put the kettle on the stove and crossed the kitchen.

"Alma and I never married," Doe said firmly. "We stayed here to take care of Mom so the boys could marry."

"Didn't you ever want to leave?"

"No," Doe said. "No, we never did. This is our home. We never wanted to leave."

Out in the living room, Anne could see Alma setting up the card table for Scrabble.

Doe turned to her. "You'll always have a home here with us, when you decide, Emma."

Anne squinted behind her dark glasses. The pool deck was dry and the cement glared in the morning sun. She sat on one of the slatted poolside benches, intending only to watch. The swimmers were lined along the pool edge, facing the water. Across the pool a tall young woman in a black bathing suit and wide straw hat was checking names off a clipboard. Her hair was pulled back with a rubber band and her legs looked firm, although her stomach sloped helplessly forward, swelling her suit like a soft ripe fruit as if she'd recently had a child.

Anne counted twenty swimmers, all girls. Some she recognized from the day before. She had slipped in unnoticed, but now Judy spotted her and began waving, poking Ginny. They grabbed each other and teetered on the edge of the pool.

Anne shook her head and frowned. The swimmers shifted restlessly in the heat. They were lined up by height: tall full-chested high-school girls next to long-stalked adolescents. The line descended along the poolside from the mature to the childishly square, ending with the under-twelves, tubby and waistless like hard new buds in their tank suits.

As Anne watched, the instructor moved down the deck and the line straightened. Sunlight reflected off the unbroken blue water, outlining their tanned limbs. The water shimmered, refracting cracks at the bottom. The smell of chlorine was strong and the ten-thirty sun scorched the air like a clean dry iron.

The swimmers tensed forward and the first girl dove; a long shallow dive. The line began to peel off, a ripple of tan bodies, one after the other—striking the water like a breaking wave. Anne could tell they had practiced. The peel was well-timed, although they had trouble emerging in stroke.

"Get those elbows up." The girl in the straw hat was running down the deck beside the lead swimmer. The line of swimmers slanted down the pool, arms splashing, hesitant, carefully watching each other.

"You wouldn't believe they've been doing this for three weeks, would you?" The tall woman was abreast of her, walking backward, watching the swimmers advance. She turned to Anne, "Hello. You must be the one who's come to save us. Bob said he finally got me some help. I'm Sue Chernak."

Anne could see her freckled face under the straw brim. The last two girls dove, finishing the long peel, and the swimmers progressed down the pool, heads high, arms splashing in the sun. The lead swimmer reached the deep end.

"Now they form a circle," Sue said. Anne left the bench, moving beside Sue, following the swimmers. The hot cement burned her soles.

The lead swimmer started to turn, wet ponytail dragging in the water, her long arms churning. The line began to circle: right arm, left arm, closing on itself.

"Jesus," Sue swore as she ran along the pool edge. "Wider, Joanie. Give them more room." She turned to Anne. "Three weeks practice! We're going to use this for the finale. We haven't even tried it to music yet."

The swimmers completed a wide ellipse in the center of the pool and faced inward, treading water.

"Look at that circle." Sue leaned forward. "What are you waiting for? Start the pattern."

Anne watched the swimmers float back. Their tanned legs were refracted and short under the clear water. The legs moved to the surface and broke the water, toes pointed to the center like brown spokes. A shifting kaleidoscope of bright bathing suits and brown arms and legs. Now the legs opened slowly, making wide V's as the pointed toes touched those of swimmers on either side. An enormous uneven star formed on the surface of the water. Some of its shorter points had scabby knees.

———

Saturday night Anne was invited out for supper. "If you come early," Sue had said over the phone, "we could block out some routines to music before Al gets home. He went to Dayton this morning on business, so he won't be home early. I've told him there's someone in town from New York. He's dying to meet you. Do you drink beer?"

"Yes," Anne had said, "I drink beer." But there are so many people in New York, she'd thought, I'm not special.

Still, her small celebrity pleased her. Most of the kids knew her now and said, "Hi," on the street. That afternoon she'd been to the public library. Ellen told her where it was, in the basement of the high-school building. Her aunts had lived in Wapakoneta all their lives and never taken out a library card. Anne registered for one using Alma's name. She had walked home under the old trees carrying her books, feeling safe, looking at large wooden houses and fretted porches. Past lawns. Over walks so old and solid that they had settled into the earth. The pavement ranged up and down. Some of the walks were sunken bricks. I'm tired of New York, she thought, no one cares in New York.

When she got home from the library, Alma was in the kitchen.

"There's lemonade in the ice box, Emma Anne." Alma had looked at the new library card. "We've never been readers," she said. "We have all the books we need."

———

Sue lived in a yellow, two-story house, wooden and narrow with gray painted floorboards on the front porch. It was not new; the trees that lined the street were enormous. All the houses in Wapakoneta have porches, Anne thought, I like porches. She looked in through the screen door. The room was filled with furniture-store furniture, new, darkly upholstered, square and anonymous. A wooden playpen filled with toys stood on one side of the room. The rest of the furniture faced the television set, as if the large stuffed pieces were watching the screen.

Sue's probably putting the kids to bed, Anne thought. She rang the bell.

———

"These glasses were a wedding present," Sue said. She emptied a can of beer into the stemmed goblet that Anne held awkwardly. "Al hates them—they were from my mother—so they only come out for company."

In the background, the record player throbbed: *Tonight, To . . . night.* Anne was feeling pleasantly drunk. Outside, beyond the porch, the sun was going down pinkly through the trees.

"Al doesn't get along with my mother," Sue explained. "She owns this place. You see, we were living in Dayton when Christopher was born. I had to quit teaching and Al's job didn't pay enough." Sue took a swallow of beer. "Al's always been a salesman—he's in storm doors right now. Well, my family offered to give us this house. Al didn't want to come out here; he's from Dayton. I met him at a dance my second year teaching. I lived at the Y.W.— that's where the dance was."

"It's a nice house." Anne lifted her glass and looked through the cold yellow beer out beyond the screen door. "You have an enormous yard."

"Al didn't go to college," Sue said. "My family didn't like the idea of our getting married."

"I was married," Anne said, watching the sun go down behind the trees. "But I've been divorced for two years now. My aunts don't like to admit that. James teaches at Columbia." The sky was darkening and fireflies began to light in the bushes. "It's very peaceful here."

"Al hates it here," Sue replied. "There's nothing to do in Wapakoneta. You have to drive to Lima just to see a movie. And then it's never anything you'd want to see." The music switched to "Maria."

"Wapak seems a good place to raise kids," Anne said. "You have two, don't you? James and I didn't have any. Well, I miscarried once, but I don't think that counts. My cousins and I used to love Wapak when we were little."

"Well, I like living in a house," Sue said. "I grew up in a house. You don't get that in New York. I stayed in New York one summer, between teaching jobs—with three other girls. I slept on their couch. It was on West Eighty-eighth Street." She picked up a bowl of potato chips and held it out to Anne. "I liked the advantages of New York—the theater and everything—but it was terribly crowded and hot. There were a lot of Puerto Ricans on our street." Sue took a cigarette and offered the pack. "These kids want to do *West Side Story* for their water show, and they've never even seen a Puerto Rican."

Anne smiled. "But the music is awfully good. For that matter I don't suppose these kids have known many blacks. I don't remember ever seeing blacks in Wapak. Are any living here now?"

"No," Sue said, "but I shouldn't think they'd want to. Too few jobs. In Dayton half my classes were colored." Sue inhaled; white smoke rose from her cigarette in the dusk. "There's not enough work in Wapak to keep our own kids in town—especially if they've gone away to college. I guess we need some light." She got up and switched on a floor lamp. The sudden light made Anne blink. She had been feeling safe in the dusk.

"I taught school for a while," Anne said. "In New York, but only as a substitute. That was before I decided to finish my degree. I could teach, but the kids ran all over me. Subbing's tough."

"Teaching's easier here," Sue said. "I know everybody. The family still counts here. Discipline's not as hard." She picked up a tablet of white paper lying beside the phonograph. "Look, I've got half of 'I Feel Pretty' blocked out for the Juniors. The high-school girls need more work on 'Maria,' and now they want to do 'America,' too."

"'America'? That's awfully fast."

Sue blew smoke out of the side of her mouth. "They insisted. They want to plan their own swimming routines—but they spend most of the time planning their costumes. I'm going to have to step in soon."

She lifted the arm of the phonograph and moved it forward. *Make of our hearts, one heart.* . . . "This is the make-believe wedding. I promised the younger kids that they could do the wedding."

Anne listened. "At least it's slow." She stood and tried several arm strokes in the air. "It ought to be a waltz-crawl."

"Then will you direct it?" Sue asked. "We've got eight under-twelves. Both your fans want to be in it."

Anne sighed. "That Judy—but they do love the water. My cousins and I learned to swim in that pool; we went every day, too. Judy's turning into a good little diver, have you noticed? I've been coaching her." She listened to the music again. "The little kids could swim a simple procession, if they don't all want to be the bride. Aren't there going to be any boys in the show?"

Sue shook her head. "Not in the water ballet. They all want to be clowns. Those guys wouldn't be caught dead doing synchronized." She stood. "Are you ready for another beer?"

Anne nodded, "Please."

Sue paused in the doorway. "The diving team is doing an exhibition and some comic diving during the intermission. Mostly comic if I know that bunch. A lot of boys work on farms during the summer—especially when the crops come in. They practice after sundown." Sue went into the kitchen. Anne could hear the refrigerator open and close. Outside it was completely dark. Anne walked to the screen door and looked out. The air felt cool and the lighted room behind her was hot. Beyond the shadowed porch the sky was heavily spattered with late-July constellations.

Of course, she thought. But I've forgotten. The sky was always full of stars in July. When I was a Campfire Girl, we used to lie on our backs on the lawn, looking at constellations through a black cardboard telescope from Woolworth's. I never look at the sky in New York. There are too many lighted windows. The buildings channel us.

She heard Sue behind her. "I wonder if the older girls would listen to you—you've just come from the city." Sue was pouring beer from a frosted can into Anne's glass. A head of foam rose, spilling over the rim. Anne bent quickly and sipped a mouthful of suds to stop the swell.

"Sorry," Sue said.

Anne wiped the foam from her lips. "It's good and cold."

Headlights flashed against the windows as a car turned into the driveway and continued past the house to the garage.

"There's Al," Sue said. "I hope he won't want to eat right away. He's got to set up the charcoal broiler in the yard."

Anne stirred uncomfortably. Her cotton dress was hopelessly wrinkled and she was feeling light-headed. The car stopped, its door slammed, and they heard footsteps on the back porch. The kitchen screen door rattled on its hinges.

"Anybody home?" Al appeared in the kitchen doorway. He was shorter than Sue and wore a short-sleeved sport shirt without a tie. His colorless hair was clipped in a crew cut. There's Al, Anne thought, and waited for an impression.

———

"When you and your ex- lived in Greenwich Village," Al said, "tell me, did you meet any queers?" He was spreading mustard over his hamburger and pointed the yellow-tipped knife at Anne.

Anne sat on the floor near the coffee table, which was spread with picnic food: a platter of hamburgers, sliced tomatoes, deviled eggs, pickles in a jar, and a bottle of catsup.

"James and I lived in the South Village," Anne said.

"It was a neighborhood—chiefly Italian—you know, families."

Sue and Al leaned forward on the couch. Sue was dishing potato salad onto paper plates. In the corner the record player spun through Al's collection of old rock-and-roll 45s.

Al speared a tomato with his knife, dropped it onto the hamburger, and snapped the roll shut. "But what about the queers?" he insisted. "Homo*sex*uals?"

"Well," Anne looked around for her beer glass. It was on the floor behind her. "They have their own bars, 'gay' bars."

"The bars in New York are open until four A.M.," Al said. "You can't tell me things don't go on."

"I can't. Things do go on—it's New York."

She looked at Al's flushed face.

"I don't go to the Village anymore," Anne said. "I live up near Columbia now—that's a long subway ride alone at night. The IRT after midnight is my idea of hell. I don't need that."

Al got to his feet and walked around the table. "S'cuse me, Anne, I've got to go take a leak. How about another beer?"

Sue looked embarrassed. "I hope you don't mind the questions. Al's never been anywhere . . . so he's terribly curious. Nothing ever happens here." She wiped some catsup off the table. "Doesn't anyone see you home?"

Anne shook her head. "I won't let them. It's too far. If I want to see our old friends or have a drink, I know I'll have to take care of myself."

"Al would never let me do that," Sue said. "In the end I guess that's why I married him. Al takes care of me. In Dayton, he used to pick me up every day after school, because of the neighborhood. Al's not exactly educated, but he's very reliable."

The record player changed and a new 45 clicked into place.

Sue emptied a can of beer into her glass and watched it drip. "Al's very reliable."

Outside someone mounted the steps. Anne and Sue looked toward the screen door. A tall woman crossed the porch, reflected in light from the living room. She had clipped hair and wore a golf dress and brown tie shoes. Behind them, Al returned from the kitchen, carrying two cans of beer.

"Well, well," he said, coming into the room and setting the cans on the coffee table. "If it isn't our friendly landlady."

"Al," Sue warned. Her freckled upper lip stretched, whitening above her mouth.

The woman opened the screen door and walked in. She was as tall as Sue.

"Mother," Sue said, "Hi. I'd like you to meet my new friend, Anne Martin."

Anne tried to stand but her leg cramped and she ended on her knees.

"Then you must be Mrs. Martin," the woman interrupted. "Your aunts on Elm Street telephoned me just now. They didn't know my daughter's married name," she glanced at Al.

"Mom lives just down the street," Sue explained.

"Alma and Fredonia Reade," Mrs. Fuller said. "I knew your Aunt Alma when she worked at the courthouse. They seem to think you should have been home before this."

Still kneeling, Anne looked at her watch. "It's eleven," she said. She was conscious of wrinkles across her skirt and grease spots from the hamburger where her lap had been.

"Would you like a beer, Mom?" Sue asked.

Mrs. Fuller smiled at Anne. She turned to Sue, "No, honey, I haven't time. Your dad and I are playing bridge with the Hoveys. I said I'd be right back." She looked at Anne. "Your aunts seem quite upset. They said you didn't tell them you'd be out late."

"Late?" Anne managed to rise to her feet. "But it isn't late. I'm awfully sorry that you were bothered, Mrs. Fuller."

The older woman opened the screen door. "We'll see you tomorrow for supper, Sue?" she asked. The door closed and her health shoes sounded on the wooden porch.

"Good grief," Anne said. She stood in the middle of the room. "I'm so sorry, Sue. This is ridiculous. I've got a key . . . and Wapak's safe. I've been on my own for years now. All alone the last two. I always go home by myself at night—much later than this—and nobody gives a damn. Wapak's nothing compared to New York. Why some of the things I've seen in the subway would make Sodom and Gomorrah look like Disneyland."

"Hey, now, take it easy," Al said. "Have another beer, Anne. Sit down. You can't let these old Wapakoneta biddies run your life. Relax. Drink your beer."

———

Behind her a porch light flicked off, leaving Anne alone in the black-green quiet. Anne started down the walk. Overhead the dark, arched branches of trees shadowed the pavement from the streetlight. The air was still. Her sneakers sounded on the cement and she could hear insects under the trimmed grass. Most houses were dark; a few had light in an upstairs window. Anne walked steadily. I'm drunk, she thought. Fireflies lighted in the branches overhead, flickered silently, moving above the still lawns and the black shape of bushes. "Lightning bugs," she explained. There was no one in the street.

At the intersection of Auglaize and Elm streets, the traffic signal was switching colors, although no traffic waited. Anne's eyes fastened on it as she walked. The small circles changed: red: green: yellow. On the far corner someone had left a neon sign lighted in the saloon window: "Frankenmuth Beer." Frankenmuth Beer was brewed in Findlay, Ohio. Anne stopped and waited at the curb for the signal to change before she crossed in the merging arcs of two street lamps, then it was dark again. As she walked toward the black angle of the bridge she began to smell the river.

Underfoot the surface changed; her steps became hollow and metallic—she could see the dark shapes of the banks on either side. The water was not far below. Frogs bellowed across the water to each other, croaked deeply in the tall blurred grass.

Anne stopped and leaned over the rail, breathing the heavy river smell as it rose. The air felt warm and moist. I'm all alone, she thought. She looked down, listening to the water. "James," she said to the water. Her voice seemed to travel a long way downstream. The water flowed. "Damn you, James," she said. "Where are you?" The frogs stopped croaking. She could hear her voice moving downstream. Someone was crying. Anne looked downriver where the banks, dark sky, and water merged. James is asleep, she thought. She stood swaying. At the edge of the water there was a splash. Grass rustled. There was another plop directly below her, near the pilings. Anne leaned far over trying to see into the black water. "OK," she called. "Let's go, gang. Everybody out of the pool."

There was movement in the bank grass, then all was still. She frowned. "Those frogs are a stubborn race," she said and turned away from the rail. Her footsteps continued hollowly. She listened to the sound until it grew thick and solid once more—and then forgot.

The house looked dark as she approached from Elm

Street, then she saw a glow along one corner. They had left the porch light on for her. Anne crossed the soft black grass and mounted the wooden steps. She carefully opened the screen door and eased through, holding the hook, trying not to let it bang.

Overhead the hall light went on suddenly. She saw her aunts standing at the foot of the stairs. Both were in their nightgowns and their heads were covered with little gray snails of hair wound on kid curlers and tied. Exactly the same as her grandmother had worn. Alma's glasses glinted octagonally, reflecting the dim overhead light.

"Emma Anne." Alma came forward. "It's midnight. You worried us. We've been waiting up for you."

"You walked home alone," Doe said. "We saw you. Emma Anne, you can't be too careful. The fair is in town."

———

Anne woke in her grandmother's bed, feeling her head ache. Turning on the pillow she slitted her eyes, letting the bright, hot sunlight under her lashes. Alma was standing in the doorway.

"Emma, the last mass today is at ten-thirty. Fredonia and I let you sleep. We went to the seven as usual. You'll have to get up right away. It's a high mass," Alma added.

Anne felt sweat trickle along her hairline. Fibers of pain branched up the back of her neck, through her right eye, and deep into her skull like a crack. Her mouth was dry. There was no air in the room. She started to raise her shoulders from the bed and then let her forehead sink back into the hot feather pillow. Hangover, she thought, oh golly.

Alma turned and left the room.

From the wall the Sacred Heart looked down in agony and distaste at the bed.

Anne pulled herself up leaning on her arms and was suddenly dizzy. Her head fell forward; long hair covered her eyes. Good God, I'm still drunk, she thought. I've got to get out of here. Last night's dress lay over the rocking chair; she'd slept in her underclothes. Anne crawled from the bed and stepped into the wrinkled dress. Trying to pull up the zipper in back, she retched. I can't, she thought. She held onto the bedpost and slipped into her sandals. Doe's hat was on the dresser where it had been put out for her. Anne set the prickly brown nest atop her head and looked in the mirror. "Crowned with thorns," she said. Saliva rose under her dry tongue and her stomach shook. "I can't," she explained to the mirror. She picked up her grandmother's hairbrush, toppling snapshots, and tried to pull it through her tangled hair. The bristles caught in the veiling. "Can't," she said, dropping the brush. "I have to go."

At the foot of the stairs, Alma was waiting with a black Sunday missal. Its spine was misshapen with holy pictures between the pages. Narrow ribbons in liturgical colors trailed out the bottom.

"The tenth Sunday after Pentecost. You'll have to walk fast, Emma Anne."

Anne took the missal stiffly, not daring to look up, and pushed out the screen door. It swung wide on its hinges and banged sharply after her.

The dry heat burned the air around her, and as she came from under the trees onto a bare stretch, the sun reflected in glaring layers off the cement. Her eyes burned and she wished she had her sunglasses. I haven't even got my purse, she thought. She walked quickly, trying to get out of sight of the house. Her head was cracking open like split fruit under the hot circle of straw.

Jesus, Mary, and Joseph, she thought, why did this have to happen? She felt the crack widening through her right eye. Saliva was running freely under her tongue. I've got to hurry, she told herself. They won't know; I've got an hour. Sweat began to loosen in all the tight crevices of her body. Ahead she saw the bridge. Its bright metal spurs glared silver under the bright blue sky. Houses and trees stopped, although the cracked sidewalk continued upward toward the bridge. Anne turned off into the dry grass and plunged down through the weeds. Their yellow spikes scratched her legs as the ground sloped away under her feet. Fuzzy stalks of milkweed brushed her bare arms and cracked, oozing sap. The ground continued to drop and the weeds rose. She plunged on down the bank toward the river. White foamy spittle on the joints of green blades flecked her legs and wrists. Insects buzzed around her hair. She could see the brown water ahead. Anne stumbled down the bank and fell onto her knees. She crawled the remaining feet and stretched, flattening the weeds, legs slanting upward, her face inches from the water. Mud streaked the heel of her hand. Far across the river, she heard church bells ring out. Mass was beginning at St. Joseph's. Water flowed slowly past the bent bank grass. Insects rose off the weeds and swarmed above the water. She saw the brown mud lying below the surface. The bells called far above the visible waves of heat. Anne closed her eyes and vomited into the river. She was still wearing her hat.

———

On Wednesdays, they always baked. The kitchen smelled of warm butterscotch; Alma's pie was in the oven, its stiff peaks of meringue browning. Anne sat at the kitchen table; she had a bag of peas to shell. In front of her stood a colander. Her face was sun-flushed from an afternoon's swimming and her damp bangs made a cool frame over her forehead. The flat pods cracked, splitting open as her fingers moved. The hard pale peas lay in rows, hooked to their pods by tiny umbilicals. They pinged and bounced as she loosened them into the colander.

"I haven't shelled peas in a long time," she said to Alma,

who was flouring the steak for Swiss, pounding in flour with the edge of a dinner plate. Doe, home from work, was resting her feet, peeling potatoes across the table.

"I'm going to miss your cooking. In New York, I live on frozen food and yogurt."

"If you don't take care of yourself," Doe said, "you'll get sick and have to pay doctors' bills."

Alma turned, holding the floury plate in her hand. "So you're still determined to go back?"

"Yes, after Labor Day," Anne answered. "I've promised to see the show through. Only three more weeks. They need me and I've got a lot of ideas for the kids' routines. Anyway, I've always loved swimming outdoors. I suppose it's childish, but when I'm swimming I feel as if nothing has ever changed. It's just like our childhood visits. Besides swimming is awfully healthy," she added, "and summer is so short."

"It lasts too long to suit me," Doe said. "I can't take this heat."

"New York isn't a safe place for a woman to live alone," Alma said. "The things we've read. . . ." She wiped her hands on a towel. "You cause your parents anxiety, Emma Anne. Your mother is heartbroken. She isn't well and your dad is getting on. They pray for you to come home. They have no one up there in Akron."

Anne held her breath, shaking; the peas pinged furiously into the colander. "Alma, Mother has chronic sinus and lots of friends. Dad is only fifty-eight. They have each other. Look, Alma, I know I'm a disappointment to them; you don't have to tell me. Everyone is ashamed of me. I'm sorry I'm the only one. They always wanted more children, and now it looks as if they won't have any grandchildren."

Doe looked up across the table. "You can't remarry," she said quietly. "The church forbids it."

Anne's fingers moved angrily. "Perhaps if I did have a husband like Lou and Ev, you'd stop treating me like this."

"You don't act the right way," Alma said. "Leaving a good home. Why do you want to live all by yourself now?"

"I can't live at home and be my parents' child," Anne protested. "I can't fill their need for grandchildren and stay home all my life—just so they can have someone to love and 'do' for. Alma, I have to make something of my own life now. I may be alone for a long time. I might as well get used to it. I manage fine."

Her aunt bent, taking the pie out of the oven. Its warm, brown-sugar smell filled the kitchen. Alma carried it to the lead sink and faced Anne, perspiring from the heat. "Your parents worry that you neglect your religion in New York."

Anne gripped the colander. What's the use, she thought. I can't tell them that I no longer believe anything. I haven't for a long time. They're the lucky ones not to go down screaming. They plan to live forever—up there with my grandmother—quietly stocking their pantry shelves against heaven. Unafraid.

"No one thinks the divorce was your sin," Doe said quickly. "James went back on his promise to the church."

"The church has nothing to do with it," Anne said. "It was my fault, too. You can't blame James." But I do, she thought. "James wasn't *Catholic,* Doe. Besides, he met someone else." Anne looked at both aunts defiantly. "I wanted my freedom," she lied. "I needed it for my work."

"Ambition is a sin," Alma said. "What makes you think that you're any better than the rest of your family? We never wanted to live in New York. We are satisfied with the lives God gave us."

"Jesus Christ, Alma . . . ," Anne cried.

"That's blasphemy and I won't have it in this house, Emma Anne. You make our Blessed Lady weep."

────────

Two evenings later, Anne stood in the kitchen after supper ironing white net between sheets of waxed paper to make it waterproof. Fredonia was stirring a pan of fudge sauce on the stove for their evening ice cream. "Be sure you clean that iron when you finish, Emma, so it won't scorch the next time we use it."

Anne nodded.

"This is costing you a lot of money," Fredonia said. Her spoon scraped loudly against the sugary pan.

"If my ideas work, Bob's going to get the Park Department to reimburse me." Anne set the iron on its stand.

"Well," Fredonia said, "they certainly aren't paying you for your time."

Anne grinned. "That's show biz."

────────

The second week in August was cold. The kids brought sweaters and shirts to wear over their bathing suits. They shivered, waiting to go into the water. Wet, their tanned skins faded and their lips bleached. Then the week before Labor Day, the weather turned hot again, and Bob called practice for seven A.M.

The first-aid room was stacked with costumes, and the older girls sat on the cots sewing fishnet stockings onto their bathing suits. They had bought big brass curtain rings at the hardware store which they planned to use as earrings. Both of the spare ring buoys on the wall were strung with tiaras of red and orange plastic roses.

"They're going to look more like gypsies than Puerto Ricans," Sue said as they left the first-aid room. "I just hope they don't sink under all that weight. Bob told me the photographer from the *Wapakoneta News* is coming to the pool this afternoon to take pictures."

Anne slid her dark glasses on over her eyes. The early reflection off the water was dazzling; the pool glimmered and the chlorine smelled fierce.

At the deep end, two boys and a girl were diving, playing the board, chasing each other, springing flat-footed. Anne recognized the girl and grinned; that imp, Judy. The child saw her and waved frantically from the high platform. They were practicing standard comic dives: the one-legged jackknife, riding the horse, dying swan. Daring each other. Anne waved back.

"It looks as if the divers got here early to grab the deep water," Sue said. "Could you rehearse your gang in the shallow for a while? I want to put 'I Feel Pretty' through another land drill anyway. We'll give the divers ten more minutes. I've called 'Maria' for nine."

Over the bathhouse loudspeaker, a phonograph needle scratched in loud decibels as the locker-room attendant put a record on the sound system.

"Ouch," Anne groaned. "That split the air." She looked up at the heat-clogged sky. "America" blasted across the pool. Children began straggling out of the bathhouse. Ginny and a child named Lucy came prancing across the hot cement, round stomachs water-streaked from a fast dodge through the showers.

"Ginny," Anne called, "can you girls bring me the top hats from the first-aid room—we'll practice swimming in them again."

Sue and the older girls were on the deep-end deck; Sue gesturing, putting them through their formations. The divers continued their manic descents off the high board. Over the music, Anne could hear the board snap and vibrate on its fulcrum. She lined her swimmers in pairs, the taller child of each set wearing a plastic top hat, and sent them swimming back and forth across the shallow end, arms moving in unison. She was at the point of dispatching someone to play their music over the loudspeaker, when she looked up.

Her trained eyes saw at once, and she was running up the side of the pool toward the deep end before she was sure it really happened: a girl's body being flung against the pool edge under the high board, awkwardly striking the cement, sliding down into the water, limp, bumping against the overflow gutter. Water closed over her head. Judy!

Anne ran. Her eyes blurred as her bare feet pressed the hot cement. At the deep end, she saw Sue and another girl dive. Anne rounded the corner by the ladder and reached the pool side under the board as Sue broke the surface, bringing Judy up with her. Water streamed off both faces.

Sue gasped and kicked, holding the child's head above water with both hands. They were only feet away. Anne dropped flat on the cement and stretched over the water to help. The second girl surfaced nearby: Joanie.

Sue carefully held Judy's chin, hands on either side of the jaw. The child's slack body floated to the surface.

Anne dropped her arms into the water to support the child's shoulders.

"Don't lift," Sue gasped. "I think she struck her spine."

Together they floated the unconscious body parallel to the pool side.

"She's broken her back," Joanie wailed, sobbing and treading water.

Anne stretched one hand under Judy's head and with the other supported her torso. Sue gripped the overflow gutter with her free hand.

One of the boy divers stretched out beside Anne to keep the child's hips afloat. Joanie held the girl's legs against the pool side.

Anne looked down at the unconscious face floating below her own. Judy's short, dark bangs washed back in the water, and her hair floated about her ears. She was a fair child, under her tan. Her eyelids were slitted and Anne could see the pupils, very black. Water beaded over the lashes.

"She wasn't down long enough," Anne said. "But, Sue, Judy isn't breathing."

Sue, inches away, white and wet, looked scared. Some of the older girls and little kids crowded in, standing over Anne.

Sue shouted to them, "Get Bob. Ellen, call a doctor."

Anne turned her head quickly. "Stay back," she ordered. She bent, remembering, and carefully opened the floating child's jaw. Judy's head bobbed in the water. Sue moved her arm to support the child's neck.

I've got to get it right, Anne thought. She reached both arms over the edge, tilting Judy's chin upward to open the air passage. With her right hand, she pinched the small nostrils between two fingers in a clothespin grip, then scrunching further over the pool side, Anne took a breath and sealed her mouth over the child's open lips. They were cold and wet. She breathed hard into the moist passage and her breath met no resistance. Take it slower, she thought. Watch to see if her chest moves. She glanced at Judy's navy-blue tank top; water floated across it and Judy's peach noseclip bobbed on its rubber band. Anne couldn't tell if the air was helping. Her own chest ached and her breathing was too fast. The sun burned her shoulders; her heart pounded against her ribs crushed into the cement. Judy's head kept floating away. Anne tried to steady it. The child's face was slippery. Her nose and forehead held traces of white cream—the thick, sticky kind lifeguards use to screen out sun. The zinc smell of it mixed with the strong chlorine and baby oil on the girl's chest and arms.

Anne lifted her face to let the air escape, then bent again. Twelve to fifteen times a minute. Count five between breaths, she reminded herself. Slow down.

In the water, Sue supported the child's shoulders, holding onto the overflow gutter. "She's taking air," Sue said, "but I had her up in seconds; it must be her back."

The water glimmered in the sun; the black shadow of the high diving board stretched out over the blue water, shortening as the sun mounted. Anne closed her eyes and tried to concentrate. Inhale, exhale. She could hear the water slosh-sloshing against the pool side. Joanie, still supporting Judy's legs, was snuffling and breathing hard.

Judy trusted me, Anne thought, I've got to keep her breathing. She opened her eyes and looked at the child's face—so close she could see drops of water lying in Judy's partly open eyes, the brown freckles beneath the tan. The eyes were wrong!

Anne felt a hand on her shoulder. Bob was stooping beside her and she saw the pant legs and sneakers of a locker-room boy.

"We're going to lift her, Anne," Bob said. "Keep her back straight. We've got to get her out of the water."

Anne nodded and breathed into the mouth between her hands.

"I'll give you the signal when we're ready." Bob slid his arms underwater beneath the girl's shoulders.

The locker-room boy and one of the divers were getting their arms into position further down—the body moved in the water.

Anne clutched the upturned chin, feeling her mouth slide away, breaking the seal. She lifted her head to let air escape.

"Now," Bob said. They bent and hoisted. Anne let go quickly and slid back, scraping her chest on the cement. The boys lifted Judy out of the pool. She sagged slightly and her head rolled to the side as they lay her flat on the deck.

Anne pushed in quickly, straightening Judy's head and lifting her small chin. She had counted to seven already.

Anne sealed her mouth over Judy's open lips, forcing in air. The child's wet face was touching her own; a drop of blood oozed out of the corner of one eye. God, Anne thought, internal. She looked quickly at the ears. No blood. But her fingers were staining around Judy's nostrils. Bob, kneeling beside her, was taking Judy's pulse. Anne heard him send the locker-room attendant for blankets. Sue and Joanie were swimming toward the ladder. Anne raised her face: "A doctor?" and resumed resuscitation.

"They're on the phone," Bob said. "Look, Anne, we're going to need the ambulance. Can you keep it up for a few more minutes? I'll be right back." She could hear him run down the deck.

Anne glanced up. The children were still standing back along the poolside watching; Ginny was crying. Sue and Joanie were comforting them. Anne closed her eyes against the glare of the water; sun pressed hotly on her back.

Sue knelt by Anne. "Ginny says she's her cousin. Joanie's gone to call the family."

Anne looked at the pale face between her hands, but there was no sign. Behind her, the boys returned with some blankets. Anne moved mechanically, beginning to feel dizzy from exhaling too forcefully. Her ears rang and the light fragmented across the bright water. She closed her eyes again to concentrate. How much time had passed?

Sue moved about, covering Judy with blankets, wrapping them around her legs, pulling them up over the wet chest and shoulders. Anne opened her eyes. The red drop in the child's eye was growing, congealing into a single bright tear. Anne's fingers on the nostrils were sticky.

Sue knelt beside Anne, watching Judy for signs. Inhale, exhale. She heard Sue move.

"Jesus," Sue said.

Anne looked up—the sunlight broke into grains and

cleared. A priest was approaching, walking quickly up the side of the pool: bareheaded, white collar, black suit absorbing the sun.

"We need a doctor," Anne said, and forced air down the unresisting young throat. Under the blanket, Judy's chest rose. Anne lifted her head again and pleaded, "Get a doctor."

One of the divers, still watching, took her plea for an order and ran toward the locker room to check. Bob was hurrying up the pool deck behind the priest. Anne kept her eyes fixed on the water, trying not to see the blood oozing, so close, from the orifices of the washed, childish face.

Sue moved away as the priest knelt beside the child's head, opening a small pouch. He leaned over and Anne saw his face: sallow with thinning hair and large ears. Their eyes met and Anne glared. "Don't move her," she said, and returned her mouth to the child's open lips. Out of one eye she could see that his black knees were getting wet on the cement. Inhale, exhale.

Now the priest's hand moved near her eyes. Anne saw his black sleeve and hairy wrist. His thumb was bright and gleaming, and she could smell olive oil. The thumb hovered and made a cross on Judy's forehead, marking the white cream, blending chrism with zinc oxide. They did not mix. He can't anoint her mouth, Anne thought, I won't let him. The priest was muttering rapidly. His knees were soaked.

Anne raised her head. "We need a doctor," she insisted.

Bob was standing beside the priest. He knelt by Anne's side. "Doc Hauser is coming, Anne. I called the ambulance. Doc was on a house call, but we got him. He's on his way. I'll take over now." He bent close, watching the rhythm of her breathing. "Be ready after this one."

Anne nodded. Inhale, exhale . . . she lifted her head.

"Now," Bob said. She slid back quickly and Bob moved

forward, placing his lips firmly over the open mouth. Ellen slipped in beside him and clamped the nostrils shut
with one hand. Blood oozed between her fingers.

Anne stood upright. Her arms ached. The priest was
closing his pouch. When he rose, his trousers had dark
stains at the knees. Anne moved around behind Bob and
knelt by Judy's hand, carefully turning it, seeking a pulse.
The short stubby fingers with bitten nails were limp—too
cold. Anne always had difficulty finding a pulse, but her
fingers touched it: the small measured throb alive within
the cold flesh.

Don't press too hard, she warned herself. She didn't have
a watch. She turned to ask the priest, but he was walking
down the pool deck. Ginny and Lucy were running after
him; they seemed to know him. Bob's head moved rhythmically. The sun beat down. Time throbbed under her fingers. People had begun to appear outside the wire pool
fence and she wondered where they came from. Cars were
stopping behind the bathhouse. She heard their doors
slamming. Judy's chest moved silently under the sunny
blankets.

Ellen knelt, eyes fixed on Bob, trying not to look at the
blood seeping between her fingers. Beyond them the ex-
panse of aqua water stretched, empty, clean, and innocent;
shading pale toward the bathhouse.

How long? Judy's pulse seemed faint. Anne relaxed her
fingers and found it again. The shadow of the diving board
shortened toward noon.

She saw the doctor come through the locker-room
door. He was in his shirtsleeves, carrying a satchel. Joanie
and the locker-room boy ran beside him as he strode up
the pool deck.

"Bob," Anne said, "the doctor's here." She lay the
child's hand on the cement and backed away to make
room.

The doctor pushed in, motioning her further back. He

put his hand on Bob's shoulder and drew him away. Ellen scurried back.

"She isn't breathing," Bob said.

The doctor motioned him out of the way.

Anne joined Sue and Ellen under the shadow of the high board staring at the doctor's back as he pulled the blankets away. She saw Judy's lips turning blue. No, Anne thought, what kind of a doctor is he? She started to move forward, but the doctor had seen enough. He said something sharply to Bob, who knelt and resumed resuscitation.

Beyond the wire fence they saw an ambulance pull up on the grass, and a locker-room boy was opening the equipment gates.

Anne watched as two attendants, also in shirt-sleeves, carefully unloaded the wheeled stretcher and the inhalator with its oxygen tank, guiding them through the open gates. There were crowds outside the fence now. People had followed the ambulance.

"They couldn't get hold of her mother," Sue said to Anne. "Joanie called but there was no answer. They finally got her dad, but he works over in Sidney."

The attendants lifted Judy onto the stretcher and placed the mask of the inhalator over her mouth and nose. Bob walked along with the men helping to guide the stretcher out and into the ambulance. The doctor, holding his satchel, climbed in back.

"It looks like a hearse," Anne said. The ambulance was dark gray.

"It's not the hearse," Sue said. "But it does belong to the funeral home. The fire department uses it in emergencies. It takes too long to get an ambulance from the hospital in Lima. We need a hospital. . . ."

They stared after the ambulance as it drove out of sight. Bob closed and padlocked the gates. He looked tired as he came over and took Ellen's arm.

"Doc said she struck her head. It's probably a concussion. She's good and knocked out, but he can't tell anything until they take X rays. He can't tell how bad."

I should have known, Anne thought. Judy's eyes were too black. Her pupils shouldn't have dilated in the sun. They were all wrong. Aloud she said, "Then we couldn't have done anything for Judy, even if we had known. It wasn't drowning."

"No," Bob said. "We couldn't have done a thing. We kept her breathing." They walked along the dry cement. Bob put his arm around Ellen. Outside, the onlookers began to drift away.

———

Doe was already home for lunch when Anne walked in. Alma stood at the lead sink, slicing tomatoes. The kitchen table was set. Anne slid into her place at the table. Past Alma, out the back screen door, she could see the midday sun shining on the gray cellar door and the stone cistern cover. In the yard there was a hot, rectangular garden of marigolds, zinnias, and phlox that her grandmother had planted long ago. It ran parallel to the tall wooden T-posts where the clotheslines had always been strung. The weathered posts were far apart. Forty years ago, they had been a large family.

Doe sat down and unfolded her napkin. "Emma Anne, they say that the little Haines girl almost drowned this morning at the swimming pool. The Farley child, whose mother works in packing, was at the pool. She called her mother at the factory."

Anne looked at her aunt. "It wasn't a drowning," she said. "I was there. It was a diving accident. Judy was clowning and slipped off the board; her momentum carried her back against the cement. They only took her to Lima an hour ago. It took so long to get a doctor. The priest arrived before the doctor did." I was one of the people who kept Judy alive, she thought. I did what I knew how to do. The accident wasn't my fault. "It wasn't anyone's fault," she said.

Alma carried the sliced tomatoes and onions floating in a dish of vinegar to the table. "Edith Farr called us, Emma Anne. She heard in town that there'd been a drowning at the pool this morning. She wanted to know if you knew who it was."

"I saw her hit the cement before she went into the water," Anne said. "Judy was unconscious when they brought her up. We waited—it seemed like forever—for help." Anne stared at the bright, distinct flowers beyond the screen door. Tall purple cosmos with yellow centers like daisies had thrust up in patches, spiked and insistent above the zinnias. She remembered her grandmother standing behind the zinnias. Her grandmother always wore a sunbonnet cutting flowers: a limp blue mobcap, more like a cabbage than a sun shade. I was the only adult at the pool, Anne thought, and Sue . . . but Sue belongs here. There were once morning glories climbing on the clothes-posts, and she wondered what had happened to them. This shouldn't have happened here—not here. Terrible things happen in New York. I'm responsible, she thought. I wanted to go back—just for a little while—to forget everything that happened to me. I wanted to be safe again. The way I used to be. But only for a few months. They did need me at the pool. They liked me. My mistakes followed me. I bring harm. Am I responsible because they liked me? Anne looked straight at both aunts. "Mrs. Farr is a busybody," she said. "Judy Haines was alive when she was taken from the pool. I know—I had a pulse the whole time."

———

By three she had paced in and out of the house four times—laying her library book on the porch swing, walk-

ing back and forth across the flowered dining-room carpet
to the kitchen for lemonade, paging through the Sears
catalogs on the hall table. Alma was making tomato preserves. She looked up as Anne went to the refrigerator
again. The red, seedy pulp bubbled on the stove. Alma
added sugar.

"I think I'm going to walk over to the pool," Anne said,
"to see if there's any news."

"Why can't you just telephone?" Alma asked.

"I don't want to do that. The phone has probably been
ringing all afternoon. Anyway I have to get out. I feel
shaky."

"That's the way it is," Alma said. "It always hits you
when it's all over."

Anne took the long way back to the pool instead of the
river path. As she passed the thinning residential district,
houses stopped, the sidewalk ended, and a cornfield began. Anne carefully crossed the road, skirting the town
baseball diamond. Her bare feet slid on the dusty grass and
she could hear noise from the pool.

When she got there, it was crowded as usual. The older
girls were running around the locker room in their costumes; the photographer from the paper had come. Anne
had forgotten about the photographer. It seemed to her
that after the morning, he should not be there.

Bob was glad to see her. Ellen and Joanie were with him
in their stockings and tiaras. "Anne," he said, "put your
suit on and get into the pictures."

"No." Anne felt confused. "That's not why I came.
Actually I'd forgotten." Did they think she wanted her
picture in the paper? She shifted her bare feet on the
cool bathhouse floor. "I just stopped . . . Bob, I wonder if
you've had any news?"

His smile was gone. "I called the hospital," he said. "After Judy arrived. They say it's a concussion. I don't know.

That doesn't sound too serious—maybe uncomfortable as hell. Judy's father's gone to Lima. They're still trying to bring her round."

Anne breathed slowly—just a concussion—then it wasn't serious. She felt suddenly freed. Her fingers loosened; she hadn't realized they were clenched. "It's going to be all right then," she said simply. "Do you know, I've never had to give respiration before. I was scared."

Bob smiled again. "I don't mind admitting that I was plenty worried until Doc got there. Look, Anne, do you think you could round up that gang of yours with the hats for a photograph. I saw them running into the showers a minute ago."

———

At eight in the morning, the phone rang. Anne got up from the breakfast table, toast still in her hand, knowing that it was for her. The day was hot already; Doe and Alma had gone to seven o'clock mass. Anne lifted the receiver of the upright telephone on the sideboard. She was standing next to the aged cactus plant on its stand. The long rapier leaves, mottled dark green, were covered with dust. Their edges faded yellow, but the needle points were purple and thick as fingernails.

"Anne." Sue's voice sounded choked at the other end. "Judy Haines died early this morning on the operating table. She never did come to."

"Died?" Anne said. "But we thought—they told us—everything would be all right." She stared at the cactus. It looked as if it were devouring motes of dust suspended in the sunlight that streamed through her grandmother's net curtains. The green blinds were partly drawn to keep the rug from fading.

"You're crying," she said, then, "How's Bob taking it?"

"I think Bob's going to call the show. Mom said he

didn't do anything. After Judy's dad called him this morning, he just went up to his room. He's still there. Mom phoned me. I suppose everyone knows by now; this is a small town. The phone's been ringing here ever since—kids asking about practice."

"We thought she was going to be all right," Anne insisted.

"Look, Anne, I have to go. I heard the baby crying. I've got him outside."

"Sue . . . thanks for calling," Anne said. She hung up and stared at the dust suspended in the sunlight. I shouldn't have come here, she thought.

―――――

Anne set the typewriter on the front porch and sat on the swing, paging through her forgotten thesis, trying to get back into her own work. The swing moved slowly. She looked out over the wooden porch rail. The grass was low, still brown from the late-August scorch. Across the street, the big wooden houses stood silent. Anne watched them advance and retreat. Their open screened windows and shadowed doors gaped blackly at the sun. In the living room, Alma turned on her afternoon soap opera. Its nervous, perpetually troubled dialogue floated out to the porch.

Anne turned a corrected page and looked across the street at the vacant windows, wondering if anyone was watching. The pool was still open, although the show had been canceled, but she didn't want to swim. That was over. She thought about the kids and wondered if any of them blamed her. I tried to keep Judy alive, she told herself. There wasn't anything else I could do.

The dead child had been taken to Kohlers Funeral Home, her aunts had told her. She could be seen that evening. "I've seen her," Anne said. "She had freckles." She looked at the windows across the street and thought she saw a face.

Anne stood quietly and crossed the porch on bare feet. Behind her the thesis swung gently back and forth on the green swing slats. Her feet moved silently across the flaking gray wood, stepped down on the cool chill of shaded cement, touched sudden warmth where the sun began. She walked around the house to the backyard. The grass was dry and dirt sifted between her toes.

Here the air smelled of dropped pears rotting in the grass beneath the pear trees. Her grandmother's flowers, blooming in the long center patch, were faded with heat. Dying zinnias on thick stalks showed brown undersides to the sun. Parched asters bowed their withered heads. A rich fume of decaying fruit drifted on the hot air. Anne walked to the far side of the flower bed and sat on the grass, tightly clasping her knees. Why am I so scared? she thought. Sun blazed above the dying flowers and a wasp circled, drawn by the fetid pears. The dry hollyhocks were full of small insects. Anne lowered her head on her knees and closed her eyes. What's the use, what is the use? It follows me like a sin. Good no longer happens. I bring pain. She held her legs tightly, curling her toes, and forced her eyes open. The sun was dangerously bright. Anne made herself stare at the house. It stood, white clapboard lined by sun shadows, tall and worn. Long black windows, uneven steps, sloping cellar door. The light glared.

I'm losing hold. She sat hunched in the grass looking at the house. No one would know what to do. Her parents would only be hurt again, wondering why such things happened. Their prayers, she knew, were never answered. The stalks of the high flowers cast striated shadows across the grass onto her legs. She stared past the brown petals, feeling the heat that faded them. Because I lost James, I lost my family, too. I injure people, and now I've killed that child. "Nonsense," she said aloud. "It was an accident." The heat shimmered on the unmoving air. I can't break down. No one would understand. No one would know what to do. There's no one to forgive me. Anne raised her face until the sun hurt her eyes.

The house stood silent in the sun; heat shone visibly above the sere flowers. Anne sat very still on the grass, clasping her knees.

———

The aunts walked her to the train. They took the back way along the other bank of the river, under trees, over the footbridge, and through a sunny field of wildflowers behind the station.

Anne had not wanted them to come. The midday sun was hot and high. Alma sweated, mopping her face every few feet, shifting the cardboard box that held the lunch they had packed for her. Doe walked sturdily along the dirt path, toeing out in her white health shoes, slope-shouldered, carrying a shopping bag full of ripe tomatoes for Anne's parents in Akron. They came single file through a field of yellow weeds, Anne in the lead, dragging her suitcase. Grasshoppers, perched like brown buds, bowed down the wheaty stalks and sprang across the narrow path, whirring.

"Nasty things," Doe said. "Spitting tobacco. It means an early winter."

Anne pushed the dry stalks out of their way with her suitcase. The sun warmed the crown of her head. She looked back at her aunts. "There's a fable for you, Doe— the aunts and the grasshopper. Fall is here and I've nothing to show for my summer. Your pantry shelves are filled with canned pears and tomatoes against the winter."

Behind her, Alma said, "Emma Anne, I've put three quarts of pears and a glass of jelly in this box for your dad; he always liked our spiced pears."

Anne smiled to herself and swept at the weeds with her suitcase. She could see trimmed grass by the station house and an empty wooden bench not far from the tracks. The only other passenger was a man in a work shirt and Levi's, who waited under the station overhang. He had no luggage. Anne set her suitcase on the grass and took the shopping bag from Doe.

Alma looked at her watch. "Not a minute to spare," she said. Sweat glistened below her glasses on both white cheeks.

Anne looked down the tracks; telephone poles stretched beside the rails, their wires stringing into the horizon.

"We're sorry you wouldn't stay Labor Day to see Mary Lou and Jack. They always drive up on a long weekend." Doe wiped her face.

"It's been too long," Anne said. "We wouldn't know what to say." They could hear the train far off. Anne put the tomatoes on the bench and hugged both aunts. Doe, narrow and bony, smelling of glycerine and rosewater. Alma, shorter, a pliant roundness, the sour, dumpling smell of the kitchen. Moist. She wouldn't see them for a long time. The train rushed into the station.

"We'll pray for you, Emma Anne," Alma said.

"Yes," Doe added, "now be sure and write to us."

Anne handed up her suitcase to the conductor and grasped the metal rail. Doe gave her the shopping bag and lunch.

"Give our love to your mom and dad."

Inside, the train smelled of hard candy and plush. Anne found an empty seat by a window and hoisted the suitcase above it, then looked out the streaked glass. As the train pulled away, both aunts were waving. She watched them diminish, standing there in the sunlight. The train moved slowly over the railroad bridge where the yellow river stretched along its dark green banks. She felt her throat tighten, and her eyes blurred. The train picked up speed. Anne pressed her forehead against the window and watched the river, the trees, the low buildings of Wapakoneta move away from her. 🦆

REBECCA MORRIS was born and raised in Ohio. She currently lives in Manhattan and is a speech writer at a major international bank. Her fiction has been published by *The New Yorker, Virginia Quarterly, Southwest Review,* and others.

ROSELLEN BROWN

BED

It was nice of them to offer it but, gift or not, I refuse to sleep in their bed. I'll tell you why: they hate each other.

They think it's love, and that makes it worse. They have an outdated, dangerous, maudlin conception of love that consists of abuse and abject apology—abject forgiveness, too—and I will not, my darling love, put my head on a pillow so often soaked with tears, or lay my bare body next to yours in a space that smells—I'm sure it does, deep in—of rancor and regret and the terror of letting go. Bad karma is not something you want in your bed with you.

———

I watched Nat pour a beer in Eva's lap yesterday. She yelled so loud, and tried to tear at his hair and strangle him with his tie, that he ran for the phone and called the police. Since they never arrived I assume he was bluffing, but it was enough to quiet her down. Then he tore out of the house and drove away as abruptly as a Hell's Angel on his bike, only his big slow dusty car had to grind and lurch out of the driveway and down Bottom Street and run the stop sign for effect.

They hadn't cared that I was gawking—hadn't noticed.

American Short Fiction, Volume 1, Number 3, Fall 1991

Or maybe they had and it stimulated their penchant for outrageousness. One way or another I said to her, Enough. Really, Eva, isn't that enough for you? He's crazy and he's going to hurt you one of these days. What do you know? she said. You and your gentle *boys*. She made gentleness into a far more contemptible quality than murderous self-indulgent rage. I forced myself to walk out of there and leave her to her fury, her hard exhausted breathing that sounded as if they'd just made love.

I walked toward town—we needed some supplies if we were planning on eating dinner (I suspected she wasn't but I wasn't going hungry for her, let alone for him)—and first I thought about her, or her and him—them—and then I thought about you. Eva says it is all her fault, all of it, always. If I didn't irritate him, she begins, or, What can you expect, I knew he liked this or couldn't abide that. She will cram herself into the wrong, no matter what contortions she has to get into to fit, and so she's all melted down and soaked with effort by the time he comes back needy and remorseful. Then I hear him—I've had to listen to all this sometimes, the apartment's not that big—apologize. But I haven't heard him tell her it's not his fault, he only says he's sorry it happened. Well, so am I, and so are the neighbors.

Once she thought he had a gun—a Nice Boy from Long Island this is, who'd just finished a thesis called "A Marxist Solution to the Foreign Debt," not a thug, not a rough character from a nasty neighborhood. He loved watching her cringe, or if he didn't love it he needed it. Why is it I have the terrible feeling that a part of her is enjoying the unlikeliness of it all, saying to herself, So this is what it's like to have no self-respect, to be one of those women, a moll, a Mafia wife, a soprano singing, "He's my fella and I love him," in a dark melodrama that isn't quite real. It's grown-up. It's sordid. When people write stories about scars on the psyche they're called "uncompromising" and "relentlessly honest" and the *Village Voice* annoints them with many column inches of awed approval. It puts her in touch with a whole subclass of sufferers she never gets to confront doing research in the graduate school library.

I've told you about the abortion, after which she rewarded herself with a recuperative trip to Montego Bay, so that it seemed she had only exchanged an incipient child for a good buttery tan without strapmarks. I've told you how she got a Mustang for her twenty-first birthday. She's generous with it and lets me drive it casually, without making me feel self-consciously grateful, but (perversely; I guess I have my own perversities) her very ease with this cool expensive hunk of machinery only tends to rub in our differences. She would regret it if she knew that.

So. Now she says we get along so well because you're there and I'm here and three thousand miles of empty air separate us. She stood at the mirror this morning brushing her hair a thousand times (because the secret of all her behavior is that she is a carefully-raised, finicky, well but not seriously educated middle-class daughter who still does half the things her mother taught her, from arranging frail petals of toilet paper on public toilet seats to never putting a milk carton or a jar of mayonnaise on the table, and then tries to cancel them out with behavior that would put her mother in a coma if she knew about it). So, as she brushed her straight reddish hair into a wild electrical halo, she damned us to a lifetime of decency and frustration.

You intend to be faithful, she said to me, an accusation.

Well, I should hope so. What's the sense of getting married if—

You see. You don't know anything about it, do you. You think marriage is about *facts,* about what you *do.*

And it's not? (This should not make me sound humble; I really was trying to challenge her.)

It's an attitude, Monica. Really. It's a long-range commitment to a shared existential commonality. A preparation not to be alone in the universe at the hour of your death.

She hissed out "universe" as if it were a hell we can all expect to be consigned to in the bitter end.

Really, I repeated. Is that why you were fighting about his weekend with Debra Flaherty, isn't that the name I heard? The one with the short hair and the *bust?* The chem T.A.? (I stood my ground for both of us, my sweet, I swear I did, with my hands on my hips.) Last night, I went on, you sounded like the hour of your death was upon you already, and if you weren't going to be alone in the universe it was because you were going out together. Murder and suicide. Or maybe murder and murder. *Really.*

She flipped her hair. Moments like this I wonder why I'm in graduate school, living with fools with big vocabularies. I want to work in a greenhouse, clean work, silent, big, born-yesterday flowerheads nodding at me, expressive as music and just as remote from a life of too many syllables.

Anyway, I'm writing to say that in her plans for this marriage of theirs, which seem to progress with the stubbornness of a disease no matter what is thrown in their way, she has offered us most of the battered old furniture in the apartment, which was her grandmother's. (The Orientals, however worn, their edges ragged, go with her. We'll find someplace to put them, she says wearily, sounding, I'm sure, like her mother, put-upon by the tedium of so much ownership.)

I don't mind the charity aspect of taking the scuffed dressers and the many-times painted kitchen table, which we can strip down to its original mystery wood—at this point it looks like one of those scratch-paintings on which children pick with a pin through layers of black crayon to the colors at the bottom. It's not like borrowing her car, which smacks of noblesse oblige. But, darling, the bed. . . .

If they are speaking to each other on their wedding day,

I will be a cheerful maid of honor. By the time we stand up and do our vowing, she will have been transformed into a "matron" of honor. What knowledge will separate the maid from the matron by then? Did you know that often in the late nineteenth century a woman didn't have her bridal portrait taken until well after the wedding, sometimes as late as a year later? It was, I suppose, her state, not herself, that was being recorded. Imagine the secrets she'd have borne to the photographer's studio! I hope for Eva's sake that she won't bring to our wedding the malign probabilities I see right now: Nat more careless of her feelings than he is right now, and she more desperate to please, more oblivious to her own instincts, and more convinced of the inescapability of it all.

As for us. One of the feelings I've been most astounded by is my desire to spare you pain: I feel as if, every time a blow is thrown (and they're thrown rarely enough), I want to run to receive it for you. Nonsense, Eva says. Everyone in a relationship wants power and you might as well not pretend otherwise. Nat thinks that too. You have to fight for a balance, he tells her: It's Darwinian. What kind of boxer would you make? Do you dare draw blood, go for the kill?

The kill?

Watch out, kids, Nat warns, and I want to shove his condescension down his throat. (Yes, I can draw blood but my victim won't be someone I love.) You have, he says, too many illusions, and they're the heart-breakers. He means, I suppose, that *they,* the prudent ones, have nowhere to fall from: he's already felt her flesh between his fingers when he's pinched, and had her vomit up her disgust with his taunting. (She found him on the porch at someone's party, sweet-talking a new graduate student, a tall thin girl with a sluice of slick hair like water down her back, leaning against her, a certain familiar look in his eye, "the tumescent look," Eva calls it, "swollen irises, a direct correspondence." She went into the john and got sick so that someone would call him. He came in and saw her kneeling over the toilet bowl and said, Jesus, Eva, when did you take up praying? Whereupon instead of laughing or kicking him in his nearest shin, or worse, she passed out and he carried her into the bedroom and woke her by crawling in on top of her, between the coats and purses of the party-goers. She woke crying, Rape! and he nearly suf-focated her with a striped school-colors scarf to get her to shut up. But she told me all this the next morning, proudly, I'd swear, as if they were Bacall and Bogie, and their daring indecencies sealed them in a kind of intimacy.)

Am I expecting too much, love? I feel very young beside my roommate, this woman who wants to suffer as if it's the natural next phase, just the way little girls are desperate to grow into the adult discomforts of periods and hairy armpits and pinching bras. You feel very young to me be-side her Marxist-with-annuities lover with his kick-ass glamor and the crushed Camels he's always removing, with a resigned sigh, from his back pocket, with the look of someone who's seen yet another climber fall to his death, or another horse collapse under his load. Eva likes to say, I love him for his ass, his little tiny ass, it fits right into my hands. Such bemusement. Can you really talk like that and simultaneously register your silver pattern at Lord & Taylor so that all your chaste-mouthed aunts can call forth pickle forks and gravy boats in your name?

Her father, an artist-with-annuities, was a bad boy in the Village in his time, which was the twenties. Or so she likes to say. The adjectives I associate with him (whom I never met, his liver long since tattered to lace) are "falling-down drunk" and "quick on the draw." The kind of man who, a century earlier, would have died in a duel. I suppose she's just being his little girl, maintaining the family honor. Art-ists eat the people they live with, she assures me cheerfully, in her mother's name.

As for me, she says, if I love you I'll prove it by taking anything you want to dish out. If I think her assumption is primitive, she makes it sound like honor. I've begun to have trouble breathing when I'm with her. I see these two dreadful unfamiliar people who wear our clothes and have our faces, hulking behind us like shadows, ready to eat us up without chewing.

And are there no exemptions? I ask, pretending to be ready to sit at her feet.

Through innocence to experience and out again, Eva says. That's what I was taught. Nobody just gets away with purity. She shrugs when she says this kind of thing. She sizes me up like someone she's just met, who's applied to her for something she can generously bestow if she thinks I deserve it. What makes you so damn virtuous?

Nothing. I'm not virtuous, not particularly. What makes you so eager to catch us out?

Reality, babes. I want you to face the truth.

Let the truth come and get me. (That wasn't easy to say but I said it anyway and thought I sounded frighteningly like her.)

It will, don't worry. Don't even try to imagine. He'll shock you sometime. Or you'll shock him.

This is too theoretical for me, Eva. I don't live in the abstract.

Hand in the till, all right? Hand in somebody's under-wear. Cowardice in the line of fire, some kind of fire, at work probably, I don't know. Moral corner-cutting, maybe.

Jesus, you're twenty-two years old. What's the matter with you?

A little daily arsenic, hon, and you'll never get poisoned, all right? Life's too complicated for that round-eyed stare of yours. You dumb angels. I want to see you when you give up your Good Housekeeping seal.

She smiled at me as if it were a blessing. I can't believe

we've lived together for two years, with our high ceilings and our unkillable philodendrons. If you're lucky, she says, sometime between now and later you might even get interesting.

Come to my rescue. Please. Tell me she's crude, not adult. Disillusioned, not unillusioned. Why does the negative get through, though, I do want to know that, the dirty secret, the bad fairy godmother? I remember when I played the piano the mistakes were the first things my fingers memorized and the last things they gave up.

Assure me, can you, that I'm right to tell her to give the boxspring and mattress to Goodwill, where just the promise of two—man and wife or lovers, any sex—side by side might be a comfort against aloneness. As long as they don't know her and bring down her blessing on their heads. Write or call me, sweet, but tell me I'm not crazy and, however generously offered, we don't have to take this bed we haven't made and lie in it. ❧

ROSELLEN BROWN is the author of six books; the most recent are the novel *Civil Wars* and a reissue of her book of stories *Street Games*. "Bed" is part of a series of linked stories to be called *The Wedding Week*. She teaches in the Creative Writing Program at the University of Houston.

WHAT'S NEW, LOVE?

$\mathcal{S}$ometimes, months running, Molly saw him like clockwork, two, three times a week, before the day shift took over, coming in to take his usual seat at the counter, away from the door and the draft. A little whoosh of the night air came along with him, freshening things up. When she turned to face him with the pot of coffee he would be reaching for one of the ashtrays—she saw to it he always had an ashtray. "What's new, love?" he would say, as if she knew, but even if she knew it would have slipped her mind. Molly was a big girl, as Doc called her, not the sort of waitress the men kidded around with. People could sit right beside him and not recognize him, or see anything of interest about him, but when he spoke to her they would glance up just to see if he meant it, which he didn't. He smoked too much, but anyone who knew anything knew his voice.

She first saw him in *Picnic* with Kim Novak. Her friend, Adele, who saw the movie with her, didn't think he was the man for Kim Novak, which spoiled so much of the movie for Molly she had to go alone and see it over. Long before all the men were taking off their clothes he didn't have to do more than unbutton his shirt, and let the tails hang out. Kim Novak knew that, the moment she saw

American Short Fiction, Volume 1, Number 3, Fall 1991
© *1991 Wright Morris*

him, but neither was she the right person for him, and the knowing that it wasn't going to work out saddened Molly every time she saw the movie.

The truth was, though it took her years to see it, they never really found the right woman for him, or realized he made a better loser than a winner. When she saw him at the counter, his eyes bloodshot, the swallow of hot coffee making him squint and grimace, he looked like one of the L.A. cops after a long night in the patrol car. "You get some sleep," she would tell him, and she was the one who filled and refilled his cup of coffee.

"Just a half cup more, love—" he would say, pushing his cup toward her, "—make it the bottom half."

———

From the time Molly would open the refrigerator, along with a bottle of Coke, and carry it through the house to the bathroom, her mother had spent most of the day floating in a tub of almost hot water. It pained her to walk, make a fist with her hands, move her head from side to side, or ride on buses. As a child Molly had felt that her mother's soft swollen body had soaked up most of the water she soaked in. All of her flesh was a puffy, off-white color, like bread dough, but she painted her lips and put rouge on her cheeks while Molly held her father's shaving mirror. Her bobbed hair was black. With the water in the tub up to her neck her head looked like a clown's mask. She had come to Hollywood to be a dancer, where she met and fell in love with a big studio chauffeur. Her mother's pain began soon after Molly was born, beginning at the tips of her toes and fingers, then moving slowly up her veins to grip the joints of her body. Only in a tub of water, her body in suspension, her breasts floating like collapsed balloons, was she free of the pain she could sometimes see like glowing hot coals around her joints. During the day she listened to the religious programs over the radio in the bathroom, but at night, propped up in bed, she watched the late movies.

That house had been large and airy, with a fenced yard at the back where two small dogs barked and yapped at her, but she never came to know where the water heater was, or where her husband kept the extra fuses. A big black woman cleaned it, and cooked for Molly and her mother, but her father took his meals elsewhere. Molly thought he was a soldier, and went off to the Army, because he wore a uniform and leather puttees, but he worked for the studio and drove people to Malibu, Palm Springs, and such places. When Gloria Swanson did Sunset Strip, it was her father who drove her around. After Molly and her mother moved from that house she thought her father just went on living in it. That's how dumb she was.

The house on Kansas Street, in Santa Monica, had green shingles on the sides and a chain swing on the porch. Sometimes a neighbor parked his car in their front yard. Out in front, in the curb walk, were two palm trees with tops she could see from the swings in the schoolyard, when she was swung really high. The tops were so high they cast shadows on the next block, but never on their own house. In the new house, however, her mother felt much better, and only spent part of the morning in the bathroom. Molly remembers the two of them, sitting on the bed, eating the takeout food she brought home from Doc's Place as they watched Shirley Booth in *Come Back, Little Sheba*. Her mother had said to her, Now you know what your mother's life was like.

Molly was a sunny, friendly, cheerful Irish girl with a face so broad she seemed to have no features. Everything but her wide smiling mouth was too small. At the school she was well liked by the Sisters for the way she cleaned the erasers and the blackboards. She liked to be helpful, but she didn't much care for school. Her first job in Doc's

Place, behind the deli counter, was to help make up the coleslaw and the cream cheese. She was the sort of strong, willing worker that customers got to know and ask for. "Where's she at?" they would say, meaning her. From there she went to a part-time waitress with three tables of her own during the rush hour. "How are you, Mr. Altman," she would say, since she found it natural to be respectful. They were Jewish people, mostly, from New York, used to Irish waitresses and good pastrami.

She usually knew, before most people, if he was away somewhere making a movie. What the movie was he never mentioned: she got the feeling he didn't care much for movies. How much better she got to know him, than he did her! She knew him in all the roles he had played, but he only knew her as a waitress. What took the longest time in coming to her was that being a waitress was all she was. She had once started watching a movie she hadn't finished about a poor, battered woman by the name of Wanda, her whole life so terrible that Molly couldn't bear to watch it. What she saw of her, little as it was, was like seeing herself.

It was a fact she looked better at night, her hair almost copper-colored in the light of the food warmer, but for all the way she worked, and spent time on her feet, she got heavier instead of lighter. The flesh of her arms hung loose as pouches when she reached for her orders at the service counter. She didn't take it personal, but she wanted him to know that when he said, "What's new, love?" she heard him.

Because she was the waitress most of the good tippers wanted, the younger ones felt a resentment toward her, complaining about the way she blocked the aisles during the rush hours. For everybody's sake, including her own, Doc moved her to the night shift behind the counter. It surprised her to find how much better everything looked at night, as she stood listening to the background music. Through the wide front windows she could see down Wilshire, farther than she had ever been, except to see a doctor or a dentist. If the fog was in, or it rained, she might take a cab back to her house, the TV glowing in her mother's bedroom. Leaving the TV on seemed to help her to sleep. All around her on the bed would be the coupons she had cut from the supermarket circulars, a decent, Irish Catholic woman resigned to what it was she couldn't help. What Molly tried to do, at times, was share the worst of it with her, such as what might become of Molly if she wasn't around to keep an eye on her.

If Molly was tireder than usual, and couldn't sleep, she would lie awake thinking of this fight he had with John Wayne in a Civil War movie. They fought like two blood-thirsty kids, in a gully where they couldn't get away from each other, a fight to the death. If it was a John Wayne movie she knew who would lose it. The fact that he made a better loser than a winner should have tipped her off, but it didn't. She was a sucker for a loser, and it was harder for her to cope with the roles he played than it was with him.

———

On this drizzly, humid morning she stopped to glance at the headlines on the corner rack of newspapers. There he was, smiling up at her, as if he had just pushed his empty cup toward her. It said that he had died of natural causes in this building she could see from where she stood at the counter, with a view all the way to Catalina. Joggers were passing by under the palm trees, their leafy tops lost in the mist. By some trick of the light they all seemed to be running on a cushion of air, detached from the earth. It was her deep longing to be one of them that relieved her despair. She took steps toward them, her belt buckle dangling, until the meaning of what she read came to her. He had been alone. At the very moment he had needed her the most, she had not been there.

All day long, on the hour and the half hour, she heard it

repeated, but on the late news she heard the worst of it. He had been dead, his poor dear head bleeding, for almost a week. Nobody who knew him had come to see him, or called to ask why he didn't answer. He had been drinking; he had tripped and fallen. When he cried out nobody had answered. In the rest room she had locked herself in a booth and sobbed like a child.

Was it possible for a person, for a woman, to feel worse than she felt? She stole time to sit with her head in her hands, a burden she would like to be free of. Doc put her back on the day shift so she would have more than herself to think of. What would that be? The way her tips fell off. She was no longer the person she had been, and the people who knew that didn't like it. Some of the early delivery trucks made their stops at different places, or picked up coffee-to-go in the deli. When that was pointed out to her, and it was, Doc said that what she needed was a "break." "You take a break, Molly," he said, and paid Lennie Tyler, one of the older cabbies, to keep an eye on her. "You're special, Molly—," Doc said to her, and slipped a bill into her apron pocket. One of the things she had done was change the daily menus, but he let one of his own fat girls do it, on her way to school, smearing the purple ink with her sticky fingers. Molly had her pride. She had her uses. Who else would ever know when the new cashiers took in more money than they rang up? In the mirror at the back of the pie case Molly could tell by the way they flicked their hair, cracked their gum, or avoided her eyes what they were up to. In all of her years Molly had never once cheated—until her tips fell off, and she made up the difference with her own money.

On the stormy nights Doc arranged for Lennie Tyler to escort her to her door. One night the TV light was flickering in her mother's bedroom. "It's company," he said, "a lot of people do it. There's women who can't sleep without it."

Molly might not have noticed, by herself, the way water was seeping beneath the front door. "You got a dog?" he cracked, as he let her in, the light shining on the film of water in the hallway, all the way down to the bathroom. He went ahead of Molly, sloshing the water, to push in the door. Steam filmed Molly's glasses. "You need a plumber," he said, as they stood watching the water spill over the rim of the tub, to splash on the floor. Her mother's hands, like rubber gloves full of air, were floating on the surface with her yellow wig.

"Where's your phone, kid," Lennie said, as if he had just heard it ringing, and that was all that Molly remembered before she passed out.

Whatever there was left for her to feel, she felt, but it wasn't much after the funeral, or the questions nobody could answer. How had she got herself, weak as she was, into water so hot it almost cooked her, and why was the phone in her bedroom off the hook? Molly had this dream about a wake so lifelike she actually confused it with a silent movie, a long line of people filing past a coffin in a hall with posters advertising *his* movies. When her turn came to look into the coffin it was *him*, she saw, not her mother, looking the way he did with Gloria Swanson.

Doc and the others advised her to sell the house and live in one of the places with people to wait on her. "If you want to be waited on," Lennie said, "I'm waiting." In his time off, on the weekends, he repainted the kitchen and put screens on the sleeping porch her mother had never slept on. Under the bed she found green food in the saucers her mother had put out for stray cats. Lennie fixed it all up so Molly could lie there and see the palms sway, way up where the rats lived. It worried her to think what they did when it rained, what they did when it swayed.

Lennie took her to the movies, when one of *his* was showing, then came by to pick her up in the lobby later. He put in a space heater, and moved the TV so she could lie in bed and watch the night baseball. Molly hadn't even known that they could play baseball at night. As they were watching *Sunset Boulevard* on the TV, he leaned over to whisper, "You were sweet on him once, weren't you?" which startled her more than it should have. What business was it of his who she was sweet on? "You know what you need?" he went on, sticking her with his elbow, "You need a new boyfriend!"

All this time he had been such a fool he didn't know that she had one, and would never give him up. In the movie Gloria Swanson had said it was the pictures that had got small, not her, and that's how it had been with Molly. When it was time for him to say—and one day it would be—"What's new, love?" she would tell him. Not that he didn't know, but the time hadn't come for her to say. &

WRIGHT MORRIS was born in 1910 in Central City, Nebraska, and currently lives in Mill Valley, California. He is the author of more than twenty novels and collections of stories. His novel *The Field of Vision* won the National Book Award in 1957 and he was awarded a fellowship from the National Endowment for the Arts in 1986. Mr. Morris' *Collected Stories* has recently been published in paperback.

FRIEDA ARKIN

ADDERLY'S NEPHEW

The main thing Mrs. Macnamera can't say she cares for is that irritating habit Mr. Adderly has with the front door—a way of double-thumping it closed behind him, a sound that isn't natural to the door as she knows it. None of her other students does that. Each time he leaves and gives it that unpleasant double-bang she reminds herself that one of these days she'd better examine the hinges.

He's here at four-thirty as usual, pretty well prepared—the little Schubert thing is actually quite nice (he has more time to practice than most of her other students).

The secret of her success as a teacher is that she doesn't allow herself unrealistic expectations. For the past ten years she has accepted only adults. Children are a pain in the neck, she's never had the luck to get a precocious one who is serious. They hate practicing, most of them, she has no idea why by now the routine taking of piano lessons hasn't gone the way of tonsillectomies.

She *had* used to get, now and then, adolescent boys whose world of jive and rock became temporarily eclipsed in the blaze of discovery of "classical music": suddenly

American Short Fiction, Volume 1, Number 3, Fall 1991
© *1991 Frieda Arkin*

they were listening to Angel Records and Columbia Masterworks, hour-long, nightlong, and came bursting into her studio on lesson days filled with the Sturm und Drang of the *Carnaval* or the *Hammerklavier*. But all they really wanted was to knock the hell out of a piano.

Girls too. Girls! Charm bracelets, clinking rings with stones in them the size of eyeballs. And not one of them would agree to take a file to those red or brown or purple talons. She's already had a complete set of ivory keys ruined by them. No thanks. No thanks.

Give her people who are well along in years, they know what they've missed, they stick, most of them really buckle down. She doesn't give a damn how literal and stiffish they are in the head and hands. She can practically bathe in the light of their faces when they take their hands back from the keyboard after a Bach chaconne or a Chopin prelude that they've just delivered neatly and musically: the incredulous delight she sees there makes the whole thing worthwhile. Don't anybody tell her that crabbed fingers can't make beautiful music.

Most of her students hold down full-time jobs in stores and offices. She also has a graduate student at Columbia, relatively young, on his way to becoming a mycologist. And four housewives. And Mr. Adderly, who lives on Social Security and, she surmises, has a bit besides. He's the most prompt of any of them when it comes to paying at the beginning of the month. In cash. Her one fierce stipulation with every one of her students: NO CHECKS.

He's a parsonical-looking man in his late sixties, somewhat on the ugly side, though she makes allowances for the depredations of time. She's nowhere as old as he is but she's been through the age bit with herself, enough to know there's nowhere to go but down. He doesn't seem a particularly happy man, but Mrs. Macnamera—a grass widow—would ask, What man is? He has the eyes and jowls of a bloodhound and your first hope is, viewing the length of quiet misery in his face, that he must have known happier days. You hope. Because no one should go to his grave without once having packed a little happiness close to the marrow. Often, she feels sorry for him.

He's married, has a wife still living, and they have one or two sons who live far off somewhere. Colorado, one of them lives in Boulder. She doesn't remember why Mr. Adderly told her this.

He seldom speaks of his family.

Of his living room and piano, yes. He's described the room he practices in so often and thoroughly that she *sees* it, she feels she's lived in it. It has a fitted carpet, from a time long before wall-to-wall became fashionable, with a pattern of cabbage roses. The house has been in his family for three generations. The front wall curves out into a bow window with a window seat where, he told her, he used to sit when he was a boy, on a long, thick, down-filled apricot-colored cushion, and read all the Tom Swift books. An odd thing to tell a piano teacher sixty years later. But she can see him, sunken voluptuously to the eyebrows, reading. Maybe this is the one good time in his past that he can recall. Certainly nothing else he's ever mentioned has brought that kind of pink happiness to his yellow face. (*She* remembers the selfsame bliss of childhood: as a girl she'd used to lie strung across an upholstered chair, her legs over one of the arms, reading books and eating McIntosh apples by the ton. In this way she'd read every one of Arnold Bennett's novels by the time she was fifteen.) But Mr. Adderly's window seat was torn out years ago. His wife keeps the bow window filled with ferns.

He's been taking lessons from her for four years.

"Somehow or another we never had the time or money for me to study anything," he told her on his first visit. "My father was a poor man, he was in the harness business and later went into leather luggage. We never had the money for it, but the one thing I always wanted was to attend an institute of yearning." She'd looked quickly into his face for a smile at that, but he continued to sit precise and stiff in the chair near her piano, staring at the hills and valleys of the keyboard—here first and last, his manner said, to learn a new geography.

"The instrument I've got's just an old upright," he told her. "An old Mason & Hamlin, but every tuner we ever had has got real excited about it. A collector's item, they tell us. It's got a remarkable tone."

Probably a complete wreck, Mrs. Macnamera thought. "Just be sure to keep it tuned," she'd said. "Don't let your ear get used to jangles."

"It belonged to an aunt of mine was a singer. She was the first woman ever to sing over the radio station WGY. That's in Schenectady, New York."

"I don't know as I've ever heard that station," Mrs. Macnamera said.

———

He's not doing so well with the Bartók. She gave him the Sonatina, don't ask her why. It's not that the piece is so hard technically—it's the *feel*—a different thing altogether. You've got to get that gypsy feel, she's tried to tell him, but it isn't in his bones. And why should it be in the bones of a retired leather-suitcase maker of sixty-eight, seventy, who'd never touched a piano before coming to her and whose notions of piano music—from having heard cousins play—were *Narcissus* and *In a Persian Market*?

Not that she hasn't seen a couple of extraordinary things. There was the millinery designer who wasn't ready to feed pigeons yet, who came to her after blowing her entire retirement bonus on a baby grand and now wanted lessons. She'd played the piano fifty years before. Now she had an incendiary need to learn the Paganini-Liszt *La Campanella* and arthritis be damned. Mrs. Macnamera's first impulse was to say, "Forget it," but she didn't, and a good thing, too—amazingly, the old biddy had done it. She'd conquered the piece inchmeal, hanging on grimly for a year and a half, and she did it, by God. Mrs. Macnamera felt like running her up and flying her from the roof.

"I know I'm not doing so good today," Mr. Adderly says after the Bartók, which he's done miserably. Pedantically. He takes his hands from the keyboard and gazes down on his yellowed palms, holding them as though his fingers are on the verge of disassembling—she has the thought of having to pick them up off the floor. She makes a murmuring sound, thinking of how to put what she has to say.

"The fact is," Adderly says, "we're having a little trouble at home. I didn't get to practice much this week."

She's sorry he has trouble at home.

"The fact is, my wife has this nephew's come to visit." He's turned his eyes toward the window and in the afternoon light they have a look like water. "I'm afraid I have to say he's not exactly . . . you might say, he's not exactly . . . right."

She grasps his meaning immediately. Few of her present pupils suspect there's anyone living with her in the house, and no more they should. Kenny's no problem anymore. It was a different story when he was fourteen or so; she'd lost several students out of fright, though she'd assured them absolutely that her son would never in a million years do anyone any harm.

For a period there, he liked to come quietly into the room where she was teaching—swim in, glide silently to the piano before anyone knew he was there, and fix his eyes steadily on the faces of her pupils. Their eyes, as they played, seemed to fascinate him. She could comprehend their fright, naturally. She remembered how he made her own heart stand still. For he never blinked. Eyes need lubricating. How had he managed to stare like that without damaging them?

———

Her instinct is right, there's something wrong with his nephew, his wife's sister's son from Madison, Wisconsin. "She suddenly just took it into her head," Mr. Adderly is saying, "to have her sister send him for a visit."

Mrs. Macnamera waits sympathetically.

"The fact is, I'm sort of afraid of him." He examines the heavily freckled backs of his hands. His nails look like corrugated tortoise shell. "He's been hitting my piano, for one thing. He doesn't like it when I practice. He says I'm too old to be taking piano lessons."

Such a statement would ordinarily rear her back on her legs. Naturally she's heard it plenty of times. But today she says, faintly, "We both know that's not so," thinking of Kenny upstairs.

Against everyone's advice she'd insisted on keeping him at home. "The kindest thing for all concerned is to institutionalize him right now," everyone said kindly—doctors, relatives, even Mike.

"We know how you feel," her sister Edna said to her. "Don't think we can't put ourselves in your shoes. But you've got to think ahead."

She had refused to think ahead.

"You've got to realize," Edna's husband said, "that what's here today won't be here tomorrow." Their delicate way of reminding her that she would die some day.

"I don't know how to keep it from sounding cruel," Edna said. "Forgive me, darling."

Institutionalize. A metal word without a strand of flesh hanging from it. It meant Send Him Away. Her little boy. The ultimate denial of her loving need, her loving, loving need. The words could come on her at any time: In the middle of the night. An hour before dawn. While she tried on shoes at the store. They came with the food served on her plate.

"I'M NOT SENDING KENNY AWAY!"

She'd raged, flinging at them reminders of the miracles of medicine they all appeared to have forgotten. Look at the thousands who'd been suffering from diabetes only a few years back! Every one of them headed for near and certain death—and then someone discovered insulin. She'd held her ground, and now she has to give him drops every morning in his tomato juice. Her son is six feet three, a strong young giant—fortunately without a notion of what he might put his strength to. She can see Adderly's nephew taking an axe to the Mason & Hamlin, and upstairs, her half-tranquilized colossus begins to rouse and stretch.

She is fifty-two, hale, and in good health. Her hair is the same reddish blond it was at eighteen, though there's a goodish bit of gray above each ear. She looks and feels like a younger woman.

All the same, her sister said it.

———

Mr. Adderly clasps his brown hands prissily around one knee and pushes against them. He's very upset. "I *told* her not to ask him. I *strongly* advised against it."

"You think he may be dangerous?"

She guesses she's overstepped. His face, pleated and ocherous as his nails, shows something or other . . . resentment? Yes, she can read it there: See here, Madam Piano Teacher, you've never met my wife or her sister and you've never met my nephew but you're pretty quick at fleshing and blooding him, aren't you? "Well, I don't know as it's that bad," he says, so severely that she leans away from him a little. But it's as though she has her teeth into something and can't let go. Even now, after all these years, she feels there may be something he can reveal to her about this nephew of his which will have the power to make the affliction upstairs a shade less.

Now he's glancing around the room, brows contracted, looking for something safe to hang his eyes on. "The thing is, he has this terrible temper."

She waits.

"Terrible!" Mr. Adderly says. He is afraid! She thinks his hands are trembling. (Never, never does she have anything to fear from Kenny. Almost never.)

"Oh, don't practice, then!" she says breathlessly. "Maybe you'd better . . . Why don't you just wait till he goes back, why subject yourself to all that tension." Her voice so vibrates with kindliness, kindliness and compassion, that her own ears can detect it. He responds instantly:

"You know, maybe I *should* skip a lesson or so till he goes. There's no telling—the fact is, you never know what he might take it into his head to *do*."

She is looking at him anxiously.

"They've got this monastery outside Madison, big red brick place, lots of grounds. Everything very strict, you know how those places are? The Brothers wear these brown habits?"

She nods.

"Well, my nephew started sending this filth to them."

"Filth?" Mrs. Macnamera says.

"Pornography. He got hold of the names of a few of the Brothers and he kept sending this filth to them. His mother caught him at it. He's far from a child, you know, he's a man close to forty."

She sighs deeply. If her son sent pornography to monks in monasteries she'd flap her arms and crow with happiness. This one isn't in Kenny's league. Not even an infant in insanity.

"He beat his mother up when she started to cry about it. There was some thought given to having him sent to one of those places they've got, you know the kind I mean."

"Yes," says Mrs. Macnamera gloomily. "That's too bad," and indicates, by straightening in her chair, there's no reason they shouldn't get on with the lesson. Her pupil pulls himself very erect and stretches his left leg stiffly forward. Both of them can hear the knee crack. "You want me to do this one again?" pointing to the Bartók.

"I don't know that I do. You're not getting any pleasure out of it, are you?"

He purses his lips and looks at it.

"If it doesn't give you any pleasure, why bother." Her body feels the way it does after a couple of hours of gardening; she can lie right down here with her chin on the rug and poop out for an hour. But the professional reflex in her head is racing through music to find something that will appeal more to his tastes. "I think something with more traditional rhythm, some straight melody. Why don't we try some Grieg." The *Lyric Pieces*, she thinks, turning the pages in her head. The Nocturne.

She's nettled at the raw relief in his eyes, though she knows how it must be for him, Bartók on top of his current troubles. By now she ought to know better than hope to make most of her elderly students—ageable people, a cleaning woman she'd had once used to call them—get properly into Bartók, who is sublime, the other side of the Mozart coin.

She's a good teacher, and knows it. A better teacher than pianist, and a hundred times more capable than the general run. What she couldn't do if she could only get her hands on one or two really talented students! But the serious ones go into the city to study with name teachers who charge quadruple what she does. Her fingers are wide and flabby now from all the housework, wretchedly out of practice. Though she'd been headed for Juilliard once, before Mike stepped into her path. You didn't get an abortion thirty-five years ago by walking into a doctor's office.

Mike wasn't a musician, just a music-lover, he told her. He loved to listen to her play. Did she know her eyes were green when she played Schubert?

———

She writes down the name of the Grieg piece for him. "You shouldn't have too much trouble getting it, I think Cranston's carries it."

His air is so troubled that she doubts he's taken in what she's just said. He's filled with his nephew, she can see that he tastes, smells, perspires his nephew. "Look," she says, "why don't I lend you my copy until you manage to get it. If Cranston's doesn't have it they'll order it for you and it may take a while." Will the nephew tolerate Grieg better than Bartók? She gets up to rummage among her music.

Behind her he clears his throat. "The fact is, my wife talks about keeping him on. I know she misses the boys."

She's found the *Lyric Pieces* and opens the pages to locate the one she's looking for.

"I have this feeling that her sister would like that quite a lot," he says bitterly. "I have a feeling it would be quite a relief to her."

"Well, don't you let her do it." How monstrous, at their ages! That wife of his is probably senile.

Of course none of this is any of her business.

"Here it is." She takes another look at him and goes to her desk, scribbles "Nocturne, page 14" on a piece of paper and paper-clips it to the cover. You poor man, she thinks as he takes it from her. She hopes her manner doesn't show her eagerness to have him go, she can hardly wait, she needs to run upstairs on one of those searing surges of pain and love which can still occasionally overtake her, to see if she hasn't, perhaps in her mind, overblown the proportions of her son's disorder.

"Well, I guess I won't be seeing you next week then," he says apologetically, clasping the music to his chest. And leaves. Bang-bang, goes the door behind him. Well, all right, she recognizes it now. This is his way with doors. No, and no again. The only things that will obey him.

It's five o'clock in any case, time to give Kenny his game of chess before dinner. Swiftly, she goes upstairs. Chess remains the only instance of consistent thought she suspects he's willing to let her see. Years before his illness, Peter Finlock taught him chess—Pete, local master in the county tournament, who says Kenny still gives him quite a game, quite a game.

Most of the times Kenny plays with her he confers new moves on the chessmen. These he demonstrates for her in silence on the board, and when she lets him know she's got them straight they begin.

She hasn't heard a word out of him in twenty-six years.

Lately she's begun to have a little trouble keeping the moves in her mind, and sometimes during the game she can't be sure whether the moves she thinks he's just shown her aren't the ones he showed her yesterday. How shockingly closer together the days are becoming—another of those signs of age, she knows it, she knows it, the weeks accordion-pleated, her whole sense of time's passage is losing elasticity. And what's more disturbing is that sometimes he can become angry in spite of the drops, when she forgets that today he's given the rook the queen's move plus a square to the right.

What a remarkably retentive memory she'd used to have. Her brain always adapted quickly to new patterns. When she'd first learned chess as a girl, after a long session of play she entered so wholly into the architecture of the game that the entire world became a chessboard: Walking to the kitchen for a glass of water, she saw the sink as a knight's move from the hall doorway. And upstairs, her bed a bishop's move from the bathroom. She'd always felt an urgent need to castle with the two bureaus separated against the far wall.

She suspects he changes the game to make it more bear-able for himself. Because she's no match for him. But their play has become a set patch in his afternoons, he requires it now in his day as he requires his breakfast, lunch, and dinner. His own play is negligent and swift, she can't recall when he's hesitated before making a move. Yet the game remains a daily unnervement to her as she sits across from him, his body slouched and indolent, his face in its con-stant movement like a running stream. His move is ready before she's even lifted her hand to play, for she is a trans-parent player, with no guile. She knows he knows her.

There was one day when she did something on the board that infuriated him—placed herself in queen check at practically the commencement of the game, a move so ultra-stupid he could hardly be blamed for anger. What he did was throw his knight at her, cutting her on the lip. He had never done such a thing (and has never since). It must have been the sight of the blood: his face abruptly stopped its twitching, and instead his hands began to shake. She'd gotten up and run to him, taking the rumpled, contorted face between her hands. He had very little beard—to this day there's only some scanty chin hair and a little short, curly down on his cheeks. Holding his head between her hands she'd begun to cry, and leaned to kiss him. He smelled like a man, like Michael. Behind the scraggly hair she saw Michael's face exactly. "Oh God," Mrs. Macna-mera cried. Her lip hurt, she could taste the salt of his vio-lence, and suddenly she'd begun screaming at him, at him and his father, both, and in terror that she might attack her son for the monster he had become, she'd turned and run from the room, leaving him to his strangling noises.

Epilepsy, they'd thought at first, the day the sweet-eyed little boy turned in a single moment into a tiny, distorted grotesque. The seizures—they looked like uncon-trollable rage—increased. In the beginning they seemed to be brought on by any mention of a color. Why colors? No one could imagine. To tell the truth, he'd been able to recognize and name practically any color before he was three years old, even exotic ones like fuchsia and puce. Peter Finlock's doing. Pete, because he and his wife had no children of their own, set himself to educate the neighbors' little boy. He started Kenny with colors, slapping his hams and cackling when he'd point to his necktie to hear the little kid pipe out, "Magenta!" They went on to numbers, but Kenny never showed much aptitude for addition or subtraction. Then chess.

"Chess is Kenny's baby, all right," Peter said happily, and settled down to nourish the tender roots.

———

She stretches a hand forward, careful not to quite touch her bishop. Does he still retain the diagonal in today's game? For the moment she can't remember, and shoots a flurried look at her son. His face is galloping furiously as he cleans one thumbnail with the tip of the other, but she knows he's watching her. And then she recalls the move he's shown her today—bishop to move two diagonally in any direction and two to the immediate right or left. She makes her move and loses the bishop.

They've been playing about half an hour when the phone rings.

She'd had to remove the upstairs extension a few years ago, following a humiliating incident with the telephone company. They'd traced some bizarre nonvocal calls to her number, and she'd had to call the doctor in to help with the explanations. Now there's only the one phone downstairs, under the staircase. When it rings and she's up here with Kenneth, he usually refuses to let her leave to answer it. Sometimes he might let her go. . . . She thinks since the day she stood up and screamed at him that it might be students who were calling. Students! Their bread and butter! she'd shouted, Did he understand?

He probably hadn't, but she saw that her rage shook him. Her throat pulsing dangerously, she'd watched him try to catch the muscles of his face into a gnarled grin of acquiescence. Of course, whoever it was had already rung off.

Only occasionally can she allow herself a mild anger. She can love him (she often loves him) and she can be curious, still, as to what goes on in his head, as on the day she'd come to his room to find him standing before the open window, his face—for the merest flicker of an instant—absolutely still. She can't remember when, since his childhood, she'd seen his face motionless. Even so, every muscle was frozen in replica of a saturnine gargoyle she remembered seeing on the Notre Dame cathedral, on her honeymoon. She'd been well along in her pregnancy then. All that time she'd been running blissfully around Paris . . . Urbino . . . Florence . . . stuffing herself with beauty. . . .

Today it's no go with the telephone. At the first ring he raises his twitching face and in a second thrusts a hand forward and touches her king. Clear warning. She sinks the few inches back into her chair.

Later she goes down to bring him his dinner and returns after an hour to collect the plates. He is on the bed, turning the pages (but not looking at them) of the illustrated *Pegasus* Mike had bought to read to him on his sixth birthday. It's a crazy thing to admit, but she's still not sure whether her son can comprehend printed words. While his father sat beside the bed reading to him Kenny's eyes were riveted to his lips, as deaf people's are. She suspects he's probably memorized every word in this and the other books Mike read him, but she'll never know for sure.

She also has a constricting fear that one day he'll imagine he's the flying horse, and go zooming out of his bedroom window to Mount Helicon.

Her husband could never accept what their son grew into. Like her, he watched the doctors talk to the boy, tap him, prick him, draw feathers down his skin, make him walk with his eyes blindfolded. There'd been the terrible day of screams, when they'd pumped some sort of gas into his head . . . here her mind always leaps to the day beyond, after the pain. They'd taken him to Mayo, Menninger, Johns Hopkins, there was even a lunatic instant when she was ready to fly with him to a village in the German Alps after reading an article in a magazine at the beauty parlor.

After every examination each doctor spoke to them in his own manner . . . gently . . . bluntly . . . neutrally . . . angrily. The child showed brain damage, autism, childhood schizophrenia, impulse-control deficiency . . . more, more, by today she's forgotten the other terms, every one of them a heart-stopper. But for a long time Mike would have none of them. "Just listen to what the kid said this afternoon. He's just as lucid! Just as lucid!" Mike said fifty times before the boy lapsed into his final silence. And when the day came that he had to face the fact that their son was irrecoverably something, he was like a man who'd been climbing a flight of stairs that suddenly collapsed under him. For twenty-four hours he walked around like an unsouled body. He even limped. And then he joined with the rest in urging her to send Kenny to one of those places the doctors suggested. Here, he had the names on a piece of paper he pulled from his pocket.

And when she still couldn't bring herself to do it, Mike kissed her, kissed his unfathomable son, wept, and disappeared from their lives.

———

Mr. Adderly doesn't appear the next week. Well, why should he? She wasn't expecting him. No reason for him to phone, either.

Every night since his last lesson, lying in bed before falling asleep, she thinks of the nephew. What she'd really like, and she's open about admitting it, is that he turn out to be at least a psychopath. Cruel. Dangerous. Well beyond the palliative influence of four drops of Thorazine in tomato or fruit juice. She lies there, inflating the monstrousness of the old man's nephew like a painter slashing pigment on canvas. Here it is again, the magic that might bring the sleeping boy in the room down the hall to rise like a diver through the alien medium he's chosen for himself, until his head breaks water. . . .

It happens that she's rarely troubled by insomnia. She has always treated sleep negligently because it doesn't interest her. She's never sought it, all her life has slept only in order to wake. And every morning rises from a night generally thick with dreams, ready to take up the round of Anna Magdalena Bach's notebook and the early volumes of the *Mikrokosmos*.

Yet sleep does occasionally push into her consciousness, for she has one particular nightmare that infrequently comes to plague her, and she has it again the night after Mr. Adderly misses his second lesson. In this dream—she's dreamed this perhaps a dozen times—she's seated at a concert grand on a platform floating precariously high above the earth, anchored by a single thin column. What she's playing varies from dream to dream—tonight it's Moussorgsky's *Pictures at an Exhibition*—when abruptly, as it always does, the column starts to buckle. It bends, snaps, the platform upends and like a fried egg from a plate, she slides from it and goes hurtling down. The piano beside her, down they go, plunging to a Doppler effect from the tonic chord, a screaming glissando. Always, she wakes from this dream when her bed lands with a walloping thud and she lies still, forcing herself to the slow, deep inhalations she'd learned for natural childbirth.

After her last pupil leaves the next day she seats herself at the telephone under the stairs. Mr. Adderly's protracted silence makes her uneasy. The new month begins next week: should she continue to set his hour aside?

She knows before she presses the first digit that the nephew is going to stay on. Wives always get their way in matters like this. And that's going to be the end of it. He'll discontinue his lessons. The stoppage will be final. And she knows that this giving up of his one pleasure will have the same effect on Mr. Adderly as an active old man's forced retirement from a business he loves. He will die soon.

A masculine voice—not his—answers. So this is what the nephew sounds like. She tries to read in the rumbling hello some measure of the mind behind it but instead sees a tornado of ripped-out piano keys, black ones, white ones with their woody extensions, flung over the cabbage roses and lodged among Mrs. Adderly's ferns.

"I'd like to speak to Mr. Adderly, please," she says, and isn't prepared for the uncordial demand of who's calling. She dislikes the voice, as she most particularly dislikes the demand. It always suggests the possibility that her answer may not be acceptable. This provokes her into wanting to keep her identity—her name, anyway—from him.

"Tell him this is his piano teacher," she says tartly. Her words make Mr. Adderly sound eight years old.

She hears the telephone set down brutally on hard wood, and waits. The silence lengthens, and when she decides he's not even bothering to call his uncle, here he is. Mr. Adderly. And the nephew has been scrupulous with the message. "Yes, Mrs. Macnamera?" His voice sounds croaking and husky, and the dry furrows of his aged face spring instantly into her sight.

"Hello there." Her voice is jovial. "I thought I'd call and see how things are with you." She knows she sounds as though she's equated his nephew's presence in the household with a siege of illness. Well, so she has. So she believes.

Silence at the other end of the line.

"I hope you're enjoying the Grieg piece?" She can actually feel the hairs on the back of her neck rise slightly, as she can see the nephew skulking behind the piano, only waiting for the old man to dare to sit down. "Oh, how *are* things going, Mr. Adderly?"

"Well . . ." But his voice shows no strain. "I like the piece, I really do. So does my wife, we're both enjoying it. And I imagine I'll be seeing you next week, I should be able to work something up by then."

"I thought Grieg was your man. I remember thinking, probably he would appeal more to your nephew than Bartók." She laughs hungrily.

He laughs, too. "I suppose so. I didn't think to ask him. He's not very comfortable here, you know. With us. He's going back on Wednesday. My son in Colorado's offered him a job working a ski lift."

————

She mounts the stairs slowly, and opens her son's door without knocking. He's on the bed, his feet on the floor, sitting in that intimate emptiness which belongs to him and to no one else, and for a minute or two she stays there watching the kaleidoscopic play of his face.

If she's lucky she'll live to become an old woman. If *he's* lucky.

No reason not. She's strong and healthy.

He's given no sign that he's aware of her in the doorway, but now he rises and with the slight stiffness in his walk goes to the table where the chess set stands. With a shock of genuine surprise she realizes it's five o'clock. She walks to the table.

"I thought you might like to know that Switzerland is made up of twenty-three cantons," she tells him. She tosses him such random shreds now and then, never ceasing to hope that the day will come when something she says is going to catch onto one of the ratchets of his brain.

She helps set up the board. The likelihood that Adderly's

nephew has either the mental apparatus or the self-restraint for playing chess is probably zero. She watches her son attentively as he picks up a piece to demonstrate the day's new move. The queen: one square only, to right or left. No more. She smiles—he's fond of putting shackles on the queen—and nods, and they begin to play.

Now and then in one of the lightning interstices of his facial fury she can catch a glimpse of the urtext of his face—a gentle cast of eye, an undefended curve of cheek—borne into the present, uncorrupted, from childhood. She moves her pawn to K4 and says, "You know, I read the other day that very few spiders are terribly poisonous. Not even tarantulas." Imperturbably, he mirrors her move. She is always white, and usually opens with a Ruy Lopez—neither of much advantage to her, since she can't remember when last she has won a game with him.   ✺

FRIEDA ARKIN was born in Brooklyn, but grew up in a small village between the Catskills and Adirondacks in Upstate New York. She received a B.A. from The University of Chicago and an M.A. in anthropology from Columbia University. Ms. Arkin taught anthropology at Hunter College for seven years and began writing fiction after her second child was born. Her stories have been published in *The Kenyon Review*, *The Yale Review*, *McCall's*, and other magazines. Her novel *The Dorp* was published in 1969. She is currently at work on a second novel.

TriQuarterly

Fiction • Poetry • Art • Criticism

2020 Ridge Ave.
Evanston, IL 60208

$18/year
$32/2 years

DRAWING BY PETER DE SEVE. (*TQ* #56)

What do Laura Kalpakian, Robert Cohen,
C. S. Godshalk, Ron Tanner,
Barbara Bedway, Mona Simpson,
and Jayne Anne Phillips have in common?

Each writer won a Pushcart Prize with a story
first published in our magazine —
Three of those stories were lead stories
in separate Pushcart volumes —
Two of those stories also appeared in
Best American Short Stories —
And only a couple of those writers
were known to us, even vaguely,
when we took their work.

The Iowa Review

Unsolicited manuscripts
are the magic of our work.

THE IOWA REVIEW   308 EPB   IOWA CITY, IA 52242

Three issues annually, about 600 pages in all. $15 for individuals, $20 for
institutions. Add $3 for foreign mailing. Single copy: $6.95.

Name _____

Address _____

City, State, ZIP _____

☐ Check enclosed   ☐ Visa   ☐ Mastercard

Card # _____ Exp. date _____

Signature _____

For faster service, call 1-800-235-2665 to charge your subscription orders to Visa or
Mastercard

ＡMERICAN

ＳHORT

ＦICTION

Laura Furman, *Editor*
University of Texas at Austin

Contents of Next Issue, Number 4, Winter 1991

C. W. Smith	*Witnesses*
Annette Sanford	*Helens and Roses*
John Rolfe Gardiner	*The Magellan House*
Elizabeth Winthrop	*The Golden Darters*
Barry Lopez	*Remembering Orchards*
Debra Jo Immergut	*The Skirt*
Tom Piazza	*Memphis*

American Short Fiction, published quarterly in Spring, Summer, Fall, and Winter, is available by subscription. Subscriptions begin with the Spring issue.

Subscription rates: Individuals, $24; Institutions, $36 Outside USA, add $5.50/subscription.
Money order, check or credit card orders accepted.
Prepayment required.

Name _____

Address _____

_____

City _____

State _____ Zip _____

Please charge my subscription to:
_____ VISA _____ MC _____ AM EXPRESS

Account # _____

Exp. date _____

Phone # _____

Signature _____

Total amount enclosed $ _____

Reply to: Journals Department, University of Texas Press, Box 7819, Austin, Texas 78713